D0098508

THE
MIDNIGHT
ZOO

THE
MIDNIGHT
ZOO

Sonya Hartnett

illustrated by
Andrea Offermann

CANDLEWICK PRESS

Text copyright © 2010 by Sonya Hartnett
Illustrations copyright © 2011 by Andrea Offermann

First Candlewick Press edition 2011
First published by Penguin Books (Australia) 2010

Library of Congress Cataloging-in-Publication Data

Hartnett, Sonya.
The midnight zoo / Sonya Hartnett ; [illustrations by Andrea Offermann]. — 1st U.S. ed.
p.   cm.
Summary: Twelve-year-old Andrej, nine-year-old Tomas, and their baby sister,
Wilma flee their Romany encampment when it is attacked by Germans during World
War II, and in an abandoned town they find a zoo where the animals tell their stories,
helping the children understand what has become of their lives and what it means to be free.
ISBN 978-0-7636-5339-2
1. World War, 1939–1945 — Juvenile fiction. [1. World War, 1939–1945 — Fiction.
2. Refugees — Fiction. 3. Brothers and sisters — Fiction. 4. Zoo animals — Fiction.
5. Zoos — Fiction. 6. Freedom — Fiction. 7. Romanies — Fiction.
8. Europe, Eastern — History — 20th century — Fiction.]   I. Offermann, Andrea, ill. II. Title.
PZ7.H267387Mid 2011
[Fic] — dc22   2010042794

11 12 13 14 15 16 17 RRC 10 9 8 7 6 5 4 3 2 1

Printed in Crawfordsville, IN, U.S.A.

This book was typeset in Weiss.

Candlewick Press
99 Dover Street
Somerville, Massachusetts 02144

visit us at www.candlewick.com

this for laura

THE VILLAGE

If the old bell had been hanging in the steeple it would have rung to announce midnight, twelve solemn iron *klong*s which would have woken the villagers from their sleep and startled any small creature new to the village and unaccustomed to the noise. But the bell had fallen from its height weeks ago, and now lay buried in silence beneath rubble; no small creature foraged in corners, because every scrap had already been carried away in beak and mouth and paw; and no woken villagers lay grumbling, for the people, like their bell, were gone. Their homes stood ruined, their beds broken into pieces, the bedroom walls slumped across the streets. Even the steeple, where the bell had hung for centuries, had had its pinnacle torn away, so the tower now stood against the sky like a blunt unfinished question.

In the clouds above the village, the legendary black-clad horseman who is Night noticed the silence and reined in his steed, which is also black as coal. Taking his vast and circular lantern, the moon, Night brushed aside a constellation of stars and came closer, curious to discover why no bell klonged, no creature paused, and no newborn baby, woken by midnight's arrival, opened its pink mouth and wailed.

Along the cobbled streets of the hamlet, no tabby cat ran. No glass shone in the rows of shop fronts. Pots filled with geraniums had once sat beneath the streetlamps, making the village pretty; now the pots lay destroyed, and soil had spilled onto the road, and the lampposts, which had been stately, stood in the awkward angles of shipwreck masts, glass scattered at their feet. Chiseled stones which had once made houses for people and halls for officials and pillars for the market and, in the square, a pagoda to frame the town band, now lay about in ugly piles, clogging the streets and heaped against those walls that were still standing. Here and there, lazy fires burned, feeding on window frames and spilled fuel.

Bringing his great, whitely burning lantern close to the ground, Night saw a spider wandering across the stones, seeking, from amid the countless crannies, the best place to string a web; and when a cloud had passed and the light of the moon draped once more across the village, Night saw, to his surprise, two boys walking the ravaged streets.

The children stepped carefully around the rubble, their footfalls making no noise, the taller walking ahead of the smaller and deciding their path. They were younger than Night had ever been, two scraps of life with scanty limbs clad in worn jackets and boots. Their eyes in their young faces were dark, like raven eyes, and their black hair was straggly, as unkempt as raven nests; they were clearly brothers, as kittens from the same litter are brothers and remain brothers for as long as they can. Both boys carried sacks on their backs, the older bearing the weightier load, the younger charged with the more delicate. As he picked his way through the debris the small boy dared to glance up occasionally and look around himself unhappily: "Andrej," he said, but his brother ignored him and did not turn back, intent on navigating the shattered tiles and sagging awnings, the splintered timbers and toppled walls. Night watched the small boy struggle to contain himself, and fail: "Andrej!" he whispered, but still Andrej said nothing and took no notice. Something had rolled beneath his feet, tinking as it went, and he crouched to search the cobbles with cautious open palms. His fingers closed around a corkscrew: holding the find up to the white lamp of the moon, Andrej saw, silhouetted against the light, a sharp tip of iron, the snaky curves of the screw.

Tomas murmured, "Andrej," for a third, stubborn time. Andrej sighed. He knew his brother was tired, that the bag he carried was heavy, and that the desolate streets would seem haunted to him. Andrej was twelve, but he had looked after Tomas all his life, and he thought of his nine-year-old brother as a child, but not of himself as one. He strove to understand Tomas the way his uncle, Marin, had understood the rugged ponies he'd bought and trained and sold. "A horse wants to please you," Uncle Marin had said, "but it can't do so unless you tend its needs. Feed, rest, shelter, and courage!" Courage was important: Uncle Marin said, "Horses aren't fools. They like a quiet life. But if bravery is asked of them, they can be brave as gods. All it takes is someone courageous to show them what courage looks like. If you want a horse to put its faith in you, you must convince it you are fearless — Andrej the hero! — even if your courage is only make-believe." So although fear beat inside Andrej like a dark, angry bird, although every corner might conceal a soldier watching and waiting for children like them, although Marin was gone and the boys were almost alone, Andrej tried always to appear calm and undaunted for Tomas, as if the precarious life they lived was unexceptional, and held no terrors at all. He tucked the corkscrew away and said, "Come on. It's all right. We'll stop soon."

Tomas wiped his eyes with a fist and shambled after his brother. The weeks he'd spent hiding in forests and sleeping in barns and wandering windswept roads had smudged dirt into his skin and dusted the color from his clothes; probably he was hardly more visible than a shadow, but Tomas felt as brightly lit as a shrine. Andrej was right: Tomas did think the crushed village was haunted. No dog barked, no clock ticked, no tap dripped, no baby yowled, no hands clapped to chase him away from doors through which the fragrance of fresh bread was borne: but in the silence that lay like a cold sheet across the streets, Tomas heard the breathing of ghosts. Ghostly footsteps seemed to follow him, stopping at the exact moment he paused. Ghostly eyes seemed to watch him, and behind these eyes were thoughts about Tomas, about his littleness and helplessness, about what should happen to him. In their weeks of roaming, he and Andrej had passed through many towns, some friendly, some standoffish, some damaged, some untouched—but none that were eerie, as this one was. None that were so punished and abandoned and gray. In another town he would have stopped to warm his backside by one of the low-burning fires, but here even the flames seemed hostile, like jeering poking tongues. Hoisting the pack on his shoulders, Tomas hurried to catch up with his brother. "Andrej," he said, "I'm not tired. We don't need to stop."

Moonlight lay on Andrej like a fairy's suit of armor. His gaze ducked away from the wreckage to give his brother a distracted smile. "Don't be frightened."

"I'm not frightened—"

"We'll find a safe place down the road, where you can sleep."

"And what will you do?" Tomas asked it, although he knew. While Tomas slept, Andrej would return to explore the town, scouring the creaky debris for anything worth keeping. He'd climb walls and crawl into crevices, opening cupboards and upending boxes, and when Tomas woke, it would be to treasure. Once, he'd opened his eyes to a cascade of silver coins tumbling from a bead purse. Once, he'd woken to six cinnamon buns and a jar of tangy pickles; another time, to three shiny bottles of tingling apple cider. Or the treasure might be a gentleman's hat or a stuffed waterbird or a set of lead animals or a necklace made of shells, something Tomas could play with and tell stories about and even keep forever, if it wasn't too big or heavy. Tomas hugely admired his brother's courage, which brought home such bounty—but he hated it, too.

Having courage, Tomas had learned, didn't mean things would turn out well, and that you would be all right. Sometimes, Tomas knew, being courageous was the least safe thing in the world.

Since the terrible day in the birch clearing two months earlier, Tomas's life had become a challenge of endurance through which he lurched as if crossing, barefooted, a fast-running, sharp-bedded river. It was a life gnawed at every edge by worry, and the very worst worry was that one day he would wake to find that Andrej had not come back to him.

Along the street a shallow breeze blew, gusting newspaper over the cobbles. High in the sky, where the dark rider Night knelt, the wind was much stronger. A flotilla of clouds as dense as battleships was unmoored by the gale, and, when the clouds coasted across the moon, the light of Night's lantern was quenched. Darkness was thrown over the village like a sorcerer's cloak: Andrej heard Tomas whimper, and felt him catch at his sleeve.

But Andrej wasn't afraid—darkness was a friend. Uncle Marin had said, "There are house cats who sleep on doormats and sip milk from bowls. There are wildcats who live in forests, cats who can never been tamed. We are wildcat people, Andrej. You will never have a doormat, but the earth and sky belong to you." Grabbing up his brother's hand Andrej hissed, "Quickly! While it's dark! We can attack!" and the two were off, running along the perilous streets like two deer across a meadow though they had only thin starlight to guide them, dodging potholes and flagpoles and crumpling brick walls, dust devils rising and swilling black-magically in their wake. They ran laughing through the dark, and the street opened up and became an echoing village square; they swung around a corner and raced down a narrowing road where the collapsed buildings gave way to a tall and endless iron fence. Andrej let his hand jounce along the iron bars; Tomas yelled, "I'm an airplane, I'm an airplane!" and spread his arms like wings. Andrej became an airplane too, and flew beside his brother, each iron bar a solid bullet fired from his fingertips. Suddenly there was a gap in the fence, an inviting open gate: the airplanes banked, tilting their wings to dive through the gap, and there was lawn instead of broken stone underneath their feet. "Descend!" Andrej shouted, and the airplanes swooped in tightening circles before landing, roaring and coughing, on their knees. Andrej, squinting into midnight's gloom, could hardly see a thing: but he smelled leaves above him and fresh soil below, and was reminded of a forest. "We can stop here." He was panting. "I think it's safe."

The moment his words reached the air, something happened. A low rough noise, like a plank dragging through gravel, rose out of the blackness, and immediately became louder, and rougher, and nearer. It became a sound that had a word, and the word was *growl*. In the next moment, overhead, the clouds sank slightly, allowing a fringe of moonlight to touch the world. And in the light, the growling took on the shape of a wolf, rangy and tousled, with long teeth showing, standing so close that Andrej, reaching up, could have scratched its chin.

THE ZOO

Tomas screamed and scuttled backward, horrified.

Andrej, too, fell backward, forgetting about being brave. When a wolf is so near that one can see one's face reflected in its eyes, there is no such thing as courage. There is only the shrieking desire to become farther away from the wolf. The brothers yelled and scrambled, fighting against the weight of their packs to push themselves to their feet, slithering in the grass and striking their elbows and all the while remembering that a boy cannot escape a wolf, not even if he runs.

Nevertheless they found their feet and bolted, over the grass and out the gate and headlong down the street in a sightless plunge, Andrej hauling Tomas by the arm and both of them trilling wild songs of fear. They tore along the cobbles, the bars of the fence going by like a solid wall, yet Andrej heard the fall of wolf feet behind him, heard the smack of fangs at his ear, and knew that running was futile, and that he must make a stand. Shoving Tomas ahead, he wheeled — and saw that the street behind was empty, that only dust galloped at their heels, that the wolf had miraculously vanished, or had never been there. Staggering, Andrej shouted, "Stop!" and Tomas halted his helter-skelter charge instantly but apprehensively, hopping and skipping, staring about with rabbit eyes. "It's all right," Andrej promised. "Look!"

Fixed to the fence was a sign painted with purple and yellow flowers and golden fleur-de-lis; ribbony blue letters woven between the flowers announced: ZOOLOGICKÁ ZAHRADA. Tomas couldn't read, so Andrej read it for him: "It says *Zoological Garden*. It's a zoo."

Tomas wobbled in the middle of the road, blinking, looking from the sign to the road and back again. "Is the wolf in a cage?" he asked finally.

"It must be. It hasn't followed us."

Tomas remained rabbity. He knew what Andrej was going to say and he didn't wait to hear it: "I don't want to," he said.

Whatever Andrej might have replied was quashed beneath a sudden and shattering screech which should have come from some frightful mythical creature but which actually burst from the depths of the sack Tomas carried on his back. Andrej's face darkened. "Now you've woken Wilma!"

"Oh! I couldn't help it!" Tomas cried.

Andrej spun his brother, untied the sack's draw-string, and drew from its maw a bellowing wee baby wrapped in swaddling. She was bound so tightly she could scarcely move, yet her whole body emanated her outrage at the treatment she had endured, the ride on the airplane and its subsequent crash landing, the hysterical flight from the wolf. Wilma had lived most of her life in a bag slung from the shoulders of a nine-year-old boy and she was used to careless handling, but her single-note scream implied she felt they were now taking advantage of her good nature. Andrej joggled her, patted her yawing mouth, told her they were sorry and that the mayhem was at an end. "Be quiet," he begged her, for her noise was spreading out through the night like a thin sheet of steel, edgy and reverberat-ing; but Wilma, who had never lived a day without being cajoled into muteness, seemed determined to suffer in silence no more. Andrej clamped her to his chest and swung in waltzing circles, rasping, "Shh! Shh! Good baby!"; lifting one hand to the light he grimaced. "She's all wet —"

"She's always wet! She stinks!"

"She doesn't stink!" Andrej snapped, although, just then, she did. He did not like bad things being said about his sister, though he only vaguely understood why. "She's just a baby —"

"*You* carry her then!"

"Tom! I carry everything! You've only got a *baby. . . .*"

"A stinking baby," said Tomas.

Wilma arched her spine and screamed. Her mouth was a furious butterfly with pink, opened wings. Her tongue wagged like a fish tail between naked gums. No tears leaked from her hotly scrunched eyes, but dribble oozed over her chin. She drew a breath, and howled mightily again; she did not mean to forgive. Andrej held her at arm's length, amazed that someone so small could be so despotic. He imagined the rubble blown away by her noise, the last timbers of the village shaken to the ground. He imagined a soldier woken from his doze and wondering about the sound. "Get the lemon butter," he told Tomas.

Tomas removed his hands from his ears to untie the drawstring of Andrej's pack and feel about inside it, tottering on tiptoe. The pot of lemon butter was small, half empty, and infinitely precious to the boys. They did not know if babies were allowed to eat lemon butter but the sweet yellow clag was Wilma's favorite thing, and they fed it to her sparingly so it would not lose its tranquilizing power. Andrej hooked a glossy gob onto his fingertip and shoved it into his sister's mouth.

For a moment she continued to cry around the finger, immunized by her fury. But when the lemon butter touched the roof of her mouth, Wilma choked a little, and tasted—and closed her mouth around the knuckle, snuffling and looking tragically at Andrej, but helpless to protest any longer. The brothers stood on the road with their ragged heads almost touching, pondering the infant and her puce streaked face, feeling silence settle once more like a crane onto its bony nest. Wilma grunted, blew a bubble, closed her eyes and sighed. Tomas sighed too then, and felt very tired.

"Come into the zoo," Andrej said eventually.

Tomas didn't answer; he looked aside.

"The wolf is in a cage. It can't get you. There's grass to lie on. There's trees. We can give Wilma a bottle, and clean her. It's better in there than out here, on the road."

Tomas slouched. What Andrej said was true, but Tomas knew he was only saying it because he wanted to explore the zoo. And while Tomas's heart hitched to remember the wolf, he knew that he, too, wanted to investigate the zoo. It would be an adventure—and better than camping on the roadside with Wilma while Andrej explored alone. Tomas had never seen a zoo, but he had seen some things he never wished to see again from the sides of roads. "All right," he agreed, starting away with a lurch. "But *you* have to clean her."

So Andrej followed his brother back the way

they had come, the broken village whispering behind him, the baby lying laxly in his arms. The horseman of the night leaned closer as the siblings passed through the zoo's gate, and the light cast from his lunar lantern grew as radiant as its rival the sunbeams, turning the grass frost-white, icing the maple leaves peppermint, coloring the air softly pewter.

Beyond the zoo's gate, Tomas immediately lagged; Andrej, too, slowed his step, looking cautiously all around. Side by side they crossed the lawn to the place where they'd landed as airplanes. "If the wolf is free," Tomas muttered, "throw the baby to it." Andrej swallowed, saying nothing: there seemed an awful sense to the idea.

But the wolf was not free. The moon was low and brilliant enough to show them what clouds and fright had earlier concealed: that thick black bars rose up to form a cage, and that the wolf was shut behind them. The animal stood motionless in the center of its pen as the children approached, its umber eyes staring, its ears raised high. It was a large wolf, bigger than any dog Andrej had ever seen, its summer coat colored clay-red and shale-gray, its legs long and knuckly, the muzzle whiskery and sharp. It was lean, its shoulder blades jutting, the pelt lying in ripples over the ribs. Its brushy sable-tipped tail hung still, giving away nothing. Andrej, gazing at it, drew a shivery breath. How close they had come to each other, he and this wolf. Near enough to touch.

Other cages curved away from the wolf's enclosure, and doubtless they were full of interesting creatures; but Wilma was squirming against his collarbone, and Andrej's hands were unpleasantly clammy from cradling her. He set the baby in the grass and knelt to untie her swaddling. "Whew," gasped Tomas, "she stinks like murder!" but Andrej only pressed his lips. Uncle Marin had once told him that wolves were the cleverest of animals, and Andrej could feel the caged one listening to them. "She's only a baby, she can't help it," he reminded Tomas, and the wolf. "Neither of you smells good either." Which was an actual truth. He gathered up the soiled swaddling and buried it under a pile of leaves.

Tomas rummaged inside the packs for their sister's many requirements; while Andrej cleaned her with hanks of grass and dried her with a scarf, Tomas uncapped a bottle of milk and pulled a teat over its rim. They'd traded ten plaited leather bracelets for the teat and bottle, the shepherd girl bargaining hard and Andrej agreeing in desperation and reluctance, knowing the deal wasn't fair. The bottle was made for feeding lambs, and when they'd first begun using it Wilma had objected to being fed like a lamb; but she had grown accustomed now, and had possibly forgotten ever drinking as a human baby is supposed to. Having cleaned and dried his sister, Andrej shook out a rectangle of calico and folded it deftly around her bottom, securing the cloth into place with two pins. Tomas felt the usual dart of admiration when, passing the needle through the calico, his brother slipped his fingers between the baby and her diaper so any wayward pinpoint would pierce him, not her. Their mother

had done this—Andrej had learned the trick
from her—but Tomas didn't believe himself brave
enough to do the same. Just the thought of that
biting, unpredictable pain was enough to give him
the shivers. Fortunately his task was to warm the
milk as best he could, by holding the bottle against
his stomach and rubbing it with his hands.

Though it was the middle of summer the night
was faintly cool, so Andrej selected a woolen shawl
from among the rags in Tomas's pack; pressing the
baby's limbs to her body he wrapped her up snugly,
leaving only her face exposed to the air. Then he
scooped the infant from the ground and placed her
in Tomas's arms; Tomas pushed the teat into his sister's mouth before she could comment, and finally
the brothers were freed to consider the wolf.

Which stood as if carved from granite, gazing
back at them. It did not seem to breathe. After a
moment, its black nose tipped sideways: "It smells
us," Andrej was moved to say. He knew that a wolf
could detect the scent of almost anything—a snowflake fallen the previous winter, the bones of an elk

dead for years—but it was strangely wonderful to know that the animal was smelling *them.* That they had crossed over into the life of this great grave beast. "I want to pat it," Andrej realized.

"It will bite you."

Andrej knew it: he hunkered in the tangling grass, laced his fingers between his knees. The breeze blew through the maple branches above them, pushing leaf shadows across the earth. Moonlight shone on the bars of the cages like satiny snail trails. It wove into the wolf's mottled coat, sparkled on the tip of each hair. The wolf continued to stand like sculpture, but in the enclosures that surrounded it many living things were moving, sniffing, turning their eyes and licking their teeth. Andrej couldn't see this, but he felt it. Restlessly he asked, "Is she asleep?"

Tomas glanced at the baby. "No, but she's happier."

Andrej squeezed his palms together, tamping down his impatience. He didn't want his investigation of the zoo to be disturbed by further demands from his sister, so he would wait until she was satisfied. He listened to the breeze, to the sough of voices it coaxed from the fleshy maple leaves. He heard it moseying around the village beyond the wrought-iron fence, drawing sighs from crushed roofs and whistles from smashed shutters. The wolf turned an ear a little, and Andrej wondered what it was hearing. Tanks churning through burning cities perhaps, or whales talking to one another in the sea. Uncle Marin had said, "A wolf can hear your heart beating before you're even born." *Can you?* Andrej longed to ask it. *Can you hear my heart?*

"I think she's had enough." Tomas lowered the bottle. He held the baby upright and rubbed her back, not knowing why this should be done but knowing his mother had done it. Wilma sagged in his hands, kecking and gasping, and after a minute spat out a slug of milk; Tomas sopped it up with his sleeve. He wagged his fingers in her face, said, "Wilma! Little Wilma?" and she mewed contentedly. When he went to lay her in the nest of his pack, however, her eyes widened, her mouth contorted, and she gave a cry. The sound made the wolf take a step—Andrej saw twin flames of moonlight flare in its eyes. "She doesn't want to sleep," said Tomas. "I think she wants to see the zoo."

"Give her to me."

Tomas handed his sister over gladly, wiped his hands on the grass. He hoisted his baggy trousers and adjusted the belt at his hips. The jacket he wore was too large for him, and the sleeves required constant folding if they weren't to dangle beyond his hands: but Andrej was already walking away, and Tomas yelped, "Wait!" and skipped to catch up, leaving the sleeves flying like flags.

THE CAGES

The first thing the brothers discovered was that, although it was the biggest zoo they'd ever seen, this zoo was small. The maple leaves that had reminded

Andrej of a sprawling forest all belonged to a single tree which stood in the center of a circular arena of grass. Around the circumference of the grassy circle stood the cages, each shoulder to shoulder with the next so their bars formed an enclosing barrier interrupted only by the pebbly path that led back to the street. It was a place arranged like a buttercup—the rounded center, the pens radiating like wedge-shaped petals—which explained, Tomas supposed, why the zoo was also called a *garden*, despite the absence of flowers and flower beds. But at the foot of the tree, there was a green bench for sitting on, and beside the seat lolled a marble mermaid on a plinth. A visitor could sit on the bench and scan the entire zoo with just a turn of the head.

The wolf, Andrej felt, had looked at them enough: he began his exploration at the cage which stood beside the pebbled path, which was also the cage farthest from the wolf's. The children came close to the bars and looked through them. In the moonlight the enclosure seemed empty but for a faint wheaty smell, a wodge of pigeon feathers, and perches made from the branches of a fir tree; a high far corner was shielded by sheets of metal that cupped a square of inky blackness. The floor of the cage was stone — looking about, Andrej saw that all the enclosures had polished stone floors which shone lividly under the moon — and was untidily splotched and splattered. Black bars extended across the roof of the cage, and across the roofs of all the cages. Sunlight and raindrops and fog and snow could drift down into the pens, but no animal could climb upward to freedom.

Tomas had his nose pushed between the bars. "Maybe no one lives here?"

"No." Andrej felt sure that something was hunched in the inky corner, looking back at them. A sign was fastened to the bars, and he stood on his toes to study it. There were words he couldn't read, but he understood the one written largest: OREL. "It's an eagle," he told his brother.

The boys contemplated the angle of shadow. They knew now what they were looking for —

a glint of talon, a falling, lancelike feather—yet still they couldn't see it. Only the splashed floor promised that the bird was in there—this, and the fact that the iron bars formed a stalwart birdcage that not even an eagle could escape. Andrej shifted Wilma from one arm to the other. "Let's keep going."

Tomas rushed to the next cage, pressed himself to the bars. "Oh! Andrej! Look!"

They didn't need to read the sign that said MEDVED. The bear was lying at the rear of the cage, its brown chin resting on the stone, its paws curled beneath its sprawled body. Its ears were like toppled teacups, the same shape and size. Although part of the roof was covered by a sheet of decorative metal, the bear, unlike its neighbor the eagle, had no sheltered corner in which to hide: the moonlight invaded its sorrel coat electrically, made mirrors of the small eyes which glanced glassily at the children and away. It did not growl or groan. Its cage smelled breathtakingly unfresh, like an opened grave. There were wads of hay clumped about the floor, and a weed growing from a crack in the stone. In the center of the pen was an overturned pail meant to hold food or water. "That's a sad bear," Tomas realized, and Andrej agreed, "Yes, it is."

The next enclosure was crisscrossed by a network of thick ropes. Its inhabitant was waiting for them at the bars, chittering tensely. The sign said OPICE, but exactly what kind of monkey it was, Andrej could not decipher. The creature was the size of a scrawny cat and, but for an area of nakedness around its glittering eyes, equally as furry as a cat, its ginger coat sheenless but groomed. It gripped a rope with clever feet, craned its walnut-creased face to the children, and reached out a sinewy arm. Its hand was as perfect as a doll's, its fingernails tinier than Wilma's, yet there was something intimidating about that limb: Tomas kept carefully beyond its reach. "Does it want to shake hands with me?" he wondered.

"I think it wants food."

"Can we give it something?"

"Maybe later. Keep going."

The monkey raced along the ropes as they

walked by, its fearful baby face fixed on them. Halted by the bars that separated its cell from the next, it crouched with black eyes blazing, whining and grinding its fangs.

Stopping at the next cage, Tomas said, "Oohh." Although the sign read LEV as well as LVICE, there was only a lioness in the pen, lying with her thick legs folded over each other, motionless but for the tail that swished serpentinely in response to the monkey's grizzling. In the lacy moonlight she was the color of a princess's gown, a fine white-gold. She betrayed nothing of what she felt when she opened her lime eyes and saw the children staring: "How beautiful she is," Tomas marveled. Her tail continued to jump as the boys moved away, as if, once started, it was difficult to stop; but her eyes closed, and she made no further move. Her cage was dirty, and smelled wickedly. There was a brown roach running in circles at the bottom of her empty water pail. Both Andrej and Tomas noticed, but neither mentioned it.

Set into the floor of the next enclosure was a

swimming pool. The water had a moldery smell, and even in night's dimness looked green. Cruising in the murky depths was a long dark shape that seemed more liquid than flesh: reaching one end of the pool, it flipped with impossible grace and glided back the way it had come, only to flip again, and return. Back and forth the water-being swam, streamlined as an arrow, running as if on tracks, causing hardly a ripple on the surface of the water. The sign on the bars said TULEŇ, but the beast seemed something more fantastical than a seal. "Put your head up!" Tomas called. "Let us see you!" But the seal only glided steadfastly back and forth.

The next cage belonged to the wolf. It had retreated to the rear of its enclosure and stood lowering, its nose almost touching the stone. Like the lioness's and the bear's, the wolf's pen had a partial pressed-metal roof for keeping out the weather, but no concealing corner in which the animal could hide. Its uncleaned cage smelled strongly, but not as badly as the bear's. It watched the children pass by, and raised its eyes when Andrej, seeking the sign, raised his own. VLK.

The monkey was still pleading in a piercing, agitated voice. It was an unnerving sound to hear against the gray sky, the icy plate of moon, the ghostly village beyond the fence. "Can't we give it something?" Tomas asked. "Just a biscuit?"

"If we feed the monkey," Andrej answered, "we'll have to feed them all." And Tomas knew that feeding all the animals would leave nothing for themselves, and that what little they had could never fill such gigantic stomachs anyway.

The sign on the next pen announced KANEC. The cage was draped by the shadow of the maple, and though they could detect a familiar woodland odor, they couldn't see through the darkness to the boar. Andrej was struck by a feeling of unease: Uncle Marin had told him that the wild boar was almost as clever as the wolf, but much, much easier to insult—and a caged boar, famished and disgruntled, might regard boys and babies as insulting indeed. He held Wilma more securely to him, cautioned his brother, "Don't go too close." Tomas stepped back from the bars and the boys searched the gloom, but they couldn't see the animal, and moved quietly away.

A corner of the next pen was littered with small dark pellets, but the cage smelled no worse than a barn or stable. Tomas put his nose between the bars but couldn't make out the details of the creature folded against the farthest wall. "A deer? A gazelle?"

"A chamois."

"A *chamois*?" Tomas had seen chamois roasting on spits at feasts. Everybody he knew had eaten bits of one—he himself had eaten platefuls of the scarlet, spicy meat. It was ridiculous to have a chamois at a zoo—like having a *rat* in a cage, or a sparrow. He shook his head and strode on, resenting being taken for someone easily impressed. They had almost completed the circuit of cages and he hoped the last ones concealed something startling, like a dragon or a frantic crazy man who ate broken glass and chair legs, like the fellow he'd once seen in a sideshow.

LAMA said the sign: the llama got awkwardly to its feet as the children reached its pen, staring at them through heart-meltingly large, lashy eyes. Its woolly coat, a patchwork of white and russet, reminded Andrej of the blankets he'd slept under in the caravan. Its bony face, topped by tufty ears, sat high on a shaggy neck, genial, and slightly daft. "It's friendly!" Tomas decided, and slipped an arm between the bars. The llama bucked with alarm and veered away, gazing back at them grievedly from a far corner. Tomas withdrew his hand regretfully. "I only wanted to pet you."

The next cage was the last. Like the others, it had a smeared stone floor, an ornate roof of metal, iron bars across the top and around each side, and a shallow drinking tray that was stained by dried raindrops. The animal inside was the size of a sitting dog, and almost the same shape as one, except that in every aspect it was different from a dog. Its head was dainty but sturdy, like a jeweler's hammer; its front legs were twiggy while its rump and rear legs formed a muscular, meaty ball. Its tail was long and pointed, its coat the color of smoke. "What *is* it?" asked Tomas. He'd never seen such a thing.

Andrej sounded the sign out to himself before trying it aloud. *"Klokan."*

"I've never heard of that." Tomas leaned in to look. Andrej had never heard of kangaroos either, and wondered if Marin knew about them. "I like it," Tomas decided: a kangaroo wasn't a dragon, but it was pleasingly peculiar, and, for all that Tomas knew, might indeed be capable of breathing fire.

They had reached the pebbly path again, having walked the complete circle of the zoo. Wilma was sucking Andrej's thumb, almost asleep. Sleepiness weighed her down, she was heavy in his arms. He crossed the grass to the bench beneath the tree, and Tomas dawdled after him. Only when he sat did Andrej realize how footsore he was, how nice it was to sit. He arranged the baby on his knees, loosened her swaddling, sponged her drool. Tomas had stopped beside him and was looking at the cages, up at the peaceful maple, across at the marble mermaid. The monkey was still crying peevishly, but the other animals were standing and lying in a kind of resigned, silent, destitute grace. "What is this place, Andrej?" Tomas asked finally.

Andrej looked up. "A zoo. I don't think it's a fancy one. It doesn't have many animals." And most of them — the wolf, the eagle, the bear, the chamois, and the invisible boar — were not exotic, but creatures which lived wild in mountains only a few days' travel from here, animals of the kind Andrej had glimpsed occasionally during expeditions into forests with his uncle. The beasts he'd seen in the forests, however, had been quick and liquid and vital, alive in their skins; these caged ones were not like that. "Someone built it because they wanted to show how much money they had, or because they liked animals, or wanted to keep them prisoner. Or maybe the people from the village built it, so they'd have something to show visitors. I don't know."

"I didn't mean that." Tomas's birdie face twisted, struggling with what he did mean. "*Why* is it?" he asked. And what he meant was *why* was the zoo still standing, when so much had been destroyed? *Why* did this strange elegant place exist so perfect and unmarked, when shops and caravans and trees and roads and streams and whole fields, entire cities, eternal hills had disappeared? Unable to explain himself, Tomas's shoulders slumped. Lately he felt he'd been wrestling all his life to make sense of the world.

"I don't know why," answered Andrej truthfully; but why ever it was, it meant that no soldiers had ever been in this place, they hadn't trampled the grass or flicked cigarette butts into it, they had never looked from beneath the brims of their caps and seen what Andrej and Tomas were seeing. Andrej had once accompanied his father on a visit to a glassblower and the memory came to him of the glassblower's furnace, the savage fire within — and the orb of molten blue glass that the blower had spun amid the flames, the single most beautiful thing that Andrej had ever seen. "I want to touch it," he had murmured, embarrassed to be saying the words. His father had laughed his fine, warmed laugh. Andrej's heart panged now, remembering it.

Wilma gurgled, the first noise she'd made in some time, and Andrej glanced at her. And then he realized he'd only heard her because the monkey had ceased its noisy pleading for food. Looking up, he saw that the creature still hung to the bars of its cage, but it wasn't watching the children now. It was silent, and its face was turned to the sky.

Apprehension ran through Andrej like a cool, rank stream. He turned and saw that other animals were also staring at the sky. The wolf, the lioness and the kangaroo had all raised their noses to the night. The wolf's ears were drawn back so their peaks almost touched. The llama stood quivering, stamping a leg. The chamois had emerged from the gloom to stand in the center of its pen, its roan coat twitching, horns lowered to fight.

Uncle Marin always said, *An animal hears and sees and senses much more than you and I.* "Tomas," Andrej breathed, and didn't know what else to say, and had no chance to say it anyway.

The airplanes came from nowhere — perhaps from behind the broad platter of the moon, perhaps from inside a star. Against the soft gray sky they were as black and stiff as a trio of undertakers. As they crossed the space above the zoo Andrej felt the power of their engines in the core of his bones, felt his blood shaken like foam in a bottle. Side by side the airplanes flew, steady and casual but thrumming determinedly, the tips of their wings nearly touching. As they passed overhead the air seemed to flatten and gush keenly, like a great knife flung in their wake; leaves were torn from the maple tree and sent spinning like juggler's plates.

An anguished cry burst from the cages: the

eagle cannoned out of its corner and crashed explosively into the bars.

Andrej had time to clutch his sister and shut his eyes.

The air curdled pitch and filthy almost before the bombs hit the ground.

THE VOICES

Andrej heard his mother speaking. "Open your eyes. Child, open your eyes."

He wanted to do as she asked—he was so

pleased to hear her voice again, so relieved that she'd returned—but his eyes were refusing to obey. "Mama," he said, and felt a paralyzing sadness because he knew that if he didn't open his eyes his mother would leave him again, not because she wanted to, but because he hadn't seen the danger coming and protected her from it. "Open your eyes!" his mother demanded, and Andrej began to cry, because he could not.

"Kid!" he heard, and this voice he didn't recognize. It was not his father's, not Uncle Marin's, not Tomas's or his own. Someone else was near. It could only be a soldier. A soldier who knew he was hiding here, a soldier who, in this soupy blackness, couldn't be seen. Andrej sat still, hardly breathing, unable to call for help.

For a long time there was silence, an oblivion deeper than sleep.

When Andrej remembered to think again, he thought he was standing at the bottom of a well. The pit of a well would be cold and filthy and dripping, but Andrej actually felt warm and clean—warm as if sunshine had washed him, and now was cradling him. He had never felt so healthy. But the darkness assured him that he was indeed standing in subterranean depths and that his health must shortly fall away, and that he was destined to shrivel here, in the lonely saturated grave of a water well. "Mama," he whispered, needing her crucially, but his mother was gone.

"Kid!" repeated the unrecognizable voice, with an edge of impatience this time.

"Foal?" said another. "Fawn?"

"Child," said the voice which was like his mother's but was *not* his mother's, because Andrej understood that his mother wouldn't speak to him again, "open your eyes."

And Andrej saw that the walls of the well weren't made of stone but only of darkness, beyond which there was cloudy light. He sighed; his eyes fluttered, and they opened.

Ash was floating in a haze all around, a fog of parched confetti hovering from the ground to higher than he could reach. When he brushed a hand weakly through it, the haze swirled like a spirit. Beyond this ashy veil he saw the night sky, and recognized the maple branches as something he'd seen before. He was sitting on a green bench. There was grass under his feet. As the haze thinned he saw the tall iron cages, and the shapes of the animals within them. The moon was low and full and shining, just as it had been when Andrej last looked at it. He'd spent forever at the bottom of the well, yet hardly any time had passed. Tomas was still standing beside him, swaying gently. "Andrej?" he said. "What happened?"

Andrej thought he might have left his voice in the well, and was surprised when words came to his smudged lips. "The airplanes dropped bombs."

Tomas pondered this, rocking. "Why did they drop bombs?"

Andrej didn't know, and shook his head. Tomas chewed his lip for a time, then rubbed his eyes with his wrist. The drifting ash was coarse to breathe, and he coughed. "Andrej?"

"Yes? What?"

"I heard Mama."

Andrej felt scattered. Ideas and colors were swimming in his mind. When he spoke, his words sounded odd inside his head, as if he was picking each one out of a large empty box. "Me too. I heard her."

". . . Is she here?"

"No." This was the zoo, and the last place he'd seen their mother was in the hills, and the last thing she'd said to him was *run.* "She was never here."

"Oh." His brother pouted. "I thought she was. I thought I heard her say *open your eyes. . . .*" He dragged a palm down his face, and suddenly was teary. "I want Mama and Papa," he said, very small and heartbroken.

"I know," said Andrej. "I know that already."

Tomas gulped air. "Don't *you* want them?"

"Yes," Andrej sighed, and he did; but they weren't here, and wanting them wouldn't bring them, and wishing always seemed a fool's thing. Detached, he watched Tomas shed one tear and then another, and although he wanted his brother to be happy and not to cry, his truest desire was to return to sleep—to sleep as he had done in the family's caravan, deep in a pile of cushions and quilts, but to sleep on the hard old bench if he had to, because even that prospect was beguiling. He watched Tomas weeping thinly into his palms, and after some time he noticed that his brother was grimier than ever, sprinkled from head to toe with ash like a lamb chop doused in pepper. A lamb chop! The thought made him chuckle, and Tomas looked up wet-faced and scowling. "What's funny?"

"You. You're covered in dirt."

"I don't care! I can't help it!" Tomas brushed himself down furiously. "You're dirty too, you know! You're the dirtiest person in the whole *world*—"

"Child!" snapped the voice which seemed like their mother's but was *not* their mother's, and the boys went silent and looked up obediently. The lioness was standing at the bars of her cage. "The little one," she said. "You've forgotten her."

Andrej stared at the lioness. Tomas stared at her too. The instant for exclaiming in horror or astonishment came and went while the ash wafted about serenely. Andrej, not knowing what to do, looked to his lap. Wilma lay across his knees, bound fast in the shawl. She was watching him with round eyes, sucking her lip. He brushed away the soot on her face and pinched the snub of her nose, and saw she was alive enough not to like it. He looked at the lioness and, feeling intensely awkward, said, "She's all right. Thank you."

"Bring her to me," said the cat. "I'd rather see for myself."

From across the lawn came a wry bleating laugh. "I wouldn't do that if I were you, kid! Not unless you want to see a lioness eat her dinner!"

The lioness showed a glimpse of tooth. "Quiet, goat."

The chamois bounced forward. "I am not a goat!"

"Shush, both of you!" whimpered the llama. "The rumble-things will hear—"

"She *must* not call me a goat! It's disrespectful!"

"Disrespectful to goats," said the lioness, and the monkey sniggered.

"*Please* keep your voices down!" begged the llama, scanning the sky wide-eyed.

The brothers, amazed, looked first to one animal and then to another, their hearts jumping like skimmed stones. Andrej remembered something Uncle Marin once said: *Animals know things you can't imagine. And they know how to keep a secret.* Talking must be one of the things that animals knew, but kept secret. To make a fuss would be impolite, but Andrej couldn't help it. "You're talking!" he said.

"So what?" said the chamois. "Why shouldn't we? Don't you think we've got anything worthwhile to say?"

"People talk *all the time*," said the llama. "They hardly ever be quiet. They say, *Are there any more sandwiches?* They say, *Don't touch that, it's germy.* They say, *I'm not asking you, I'm telling you.* Aren't *we* allowed to talk too?"

"Well—it's just that—I've never heard of animals speaking—"

"So something is only possible if you've heard about it, is that right, kid?"

"No!" Andrej wished he'd never mentioned it. "It's just — I didn't know you could."

The chamois said pointedly, "One suspects there's a lot that you don't know."

Andrej, subsiding into silence, didn't disagree. Lately the world was proving utterly topsy-turvy to how he'd believed it to be. Tomas, on the other hand, was enchanted by this turn of events. To him it was completely understandable that the zoo's animals could talk. Locked in the cages with nothing better to do, how could they help but learn the language of the zoo's visitors? It made sense; it filled him with a giddy excitement and a renewed love for the world. To the llama he said, "We don't call them *rumble-things*. We call them *airplanes*."

"I know." The creature looked regally down its nose at him. "But I call them rumble-things. You should too. It suits them better."

"It does!" Tomas agreed happily. "Rumble-things."

The lioness was pacing, her body sweeping goldenly back and forth behind the bars. Her gaze on Wilma, however, stayed absolutely still. "The infant," she persisted. "Show her."

Tomas looked at his brother expectantly; Andrej felt the consideration of all the animals glide over the grass to him. After a hesitation in which he felt ridiculous yet compelled, he gathered his sister in his hands and held her aloft for the lioness to see. The cat's lime eyes widened, and for a long moment she stared at the infant before spinning away abruptly and slumping to the floor. Tomas gave his brother a smile that any other time would have earned him a cuff over the head; now it stirred the ash in his throat and brought on a coughing fit. "Thirsty," he croaked.

"Don't ask *us* for water," warned the chamois. "We haven't got any."

"There's nothing in the flask." Andrej had meant to fill it in the town. "We can go into the village and find a pump —"

"No!" Tomas's good cheer was doused in an instant. "Don't go out there, Andrej! It's dangerous! I'm not thirsty now."

But Andrej was curious: he placed Wilma on the bench and stood up carefully. Ash cascaded from his clothes, and swilled and spiraled in his wake as he crossed the grass. With Tomas protesting at his heels he found the smattered pebble path, and followed its crunchy length to the road.

The horseman Night raised the flame in his lamp so he too could see what the children saw.

The moonlight lay velvetly on what remained of the village. The long wrought-iron fence, where the ZOOLOGICKÁ ZAHRADA sign hung, was bent and buckled as bad teeth. The cobbled road was cratered in places, crumped into hillocks in others. The bombs had toppled the last of the buildings, including the stump of the bell tower. Flames burned higher than they had done, laying claim greedily to the new fodder of collapsed timber. Broken glass glittered on every surface, like fireflies caught in an appalling web of smashed furniture and cleaved stone. Papers and clothes were scattered through the debris, and feathers from torn pillows blizzarded everywhere. The air was smoky, gritty against the teeth, and noisy with the groaning of ruin. It *was* dangerous, Andrej saw. Not everything that had fallen had arrived in its final resting place yet. If something happened to him — a sliding plate of glass, a brightly sparking wire, a javelin-like pipe standing up from the ground, poised at the place where he tripped — Tomas and Wilma would be alone. Tomas was holding tight to his sleeve, willing him not to leave them. "I'm not thirsty," he was assuring his brother. And even in the glowing moonlight, from where he stood Andrej couldn't see a water pump. He might have to walk everywhere before he found one. Better, safer, to wait until dawn. Tomas was chirpy as he followed his brother back into the zoo, eager to put the distraction behind them. "Why did they drop the bombs?" he asked. "Wasn't the village flat enough already?"

"Maybe they didn't want to carry them any-more." Andrej shrugged. "Maybe they were heavy, and they accidentally dropped them."

"That's not the reason, Rom." The wolf spoke for the first time, and the brothers halted mistrustfully, remembering the fright the animal had given them. The beast seemed even more fearsome now that it could speak. There was no guessing what such a being might say. It knew that they were Gypsy children, and might know anything more.

But Andrej recollected his courage, and remembered that the wolf was caged. He looked it in the eye and asked, "What is the reason, then?"

The wolf sniffed loudly, as if scorningly, and sat down on its haunches. "The same reason there is for everything," it replied. *"I will have my way."*

THE REASON

The wolf said, "None of us know why your war is happening. Your squabbles aren't something we care about. When a wolf clan battles another, it's usually over territory. Probably this is the reason for your warring, but who knows? People aren't wolves."

"I wish *I* was a wolf," said Tomas.

The wolf looked at him with distaste, and went on. "We know your war is being fought everywhere, not just here in the village. We can hear it, and smell it. Birds come and perch in the maple, and they tell us that wherever they fly they see your battle, or what's left after your battle has moved on. They tell us about trucks and tents and lines of men walking from one horizon to another. They speak of tanks and torpedoes and men swooping through the sky with parachutes blooming above them. They describe grenades falling and submarines rising, and men behind wire dropping down in mud and snow. We can't see much from these cages, but we see these things."

The bear spoke up dismally. "We can't see anything except each other."

"You're complaining?" squawked the chamois. "At least you don't have to stare at that idiot chimp and the sourpuss all day!"

The lioness didn't react, but the monkey swore brutally, streaking the length of its enclosure and thumping into the bars. The chamois chortled tauntingly and the monkey flung itself about, a jungle scream sheering from its wide-open mouth. The wolf regarded them indifferently, waiting until the monkey collapsed into seething silence before looking back at the children.

"The birds say our village is different from others," it said. "They say it's the sorriest village they can see. But the invaders mustn't think it's sorry enough, because sometimes they send more planes, and drop more bombs. Maybe the village will be sorry enough when nothing is left of it, not even a hole in the ground. No earth, no air, no sky, no light—"

"No zoo," said the llama.

"No zoo," the wolf agreed.

Tomas asked, "Why does the village need to be sorry? What did it do?"

"It fought back," said the chamois lordishly.

"It fought the invaders?" When Tomas thought of the invading soldiers, he thought of the day in the clearing. He thought of stories his father had told of dark forests coming angrily to life. "That was brave."

The wolf lay down on its white belly, stretching out its legs. "Not all the villagers fought, only some of them. But to the ones who did, it wasn't about bravery. It was something that had to be done. They could not do nothing. This land was their home, their territory. They *had* to fight for it. Never mind that *their* kind have seized so much *wolf* territory, cut down our trees, set traps in our ground, caved in our dens, pursued us to —"

"Don't!" moaned the bear, turning aside its great head. "Don't talk about that."

The wolf said carelessly, "They do the same to bears. Anyway, these villagers formed a secret gang, and began to talk of vengeance. They knew they wouldn't triumph in the end — the invading clan is strong, its weapons are deadly, its numbers are countless, it's spread through this land like a creeper through a tree, and much farther than that, according to the birds: they say there's no end to the invaders, that they infest every place from sea to sea and also *on* the sea, floating, slinking — but the gang vowed that if their homeland was going to be taken from them, it wouldn't be taken easily. They knew that other people in other places were fighting the enemy too — burning crops, souring water, barricading roads, destroying firewood — but such sabotage seemed puny to the gang, the kind of mischief that the invaders would expect, as a fox expects to have fleas. The gang didn't want to be fleas. They wanted to be a swarm of wasps. They swore that, helpless though they might be to keep their territory, before it was lost they would make their enemy regret setting foot upon it."

Andrej and Tomas had sat down in the dusty grass, and Wilma, bundled on the bench, was making no sound. The brief summer night was nearing its darkest time, yet the moon still lit the zoo with a creamy light, turning the circle of cages into a place like a chapel, somewhere solemn and fragile and holy. The lioness's tail was quietly switching, and specks of ash were still wafting to earth, but nothing else seemed to move.

"A train track runs between the hills behind this village," the wolf continued. "We can hear the wheels and whistles from here. The track is important to the invaders because it leads to where they want to go, which is everywhere—every town, every hilltop, every shore. The invaders are people after all, and people are always hungry for more. The locomotives that ride the track are also important to the invaders. With the trains, the invaders can move their strength and determination and everything else an invading pack needs quickly, and in formidable amounts."

Andrej thought of geese and starlings explaining this logistical information to the captive audience at the zoo. A parrot in a cage had once said *hello* to him, and then called itself a *pretty bird*. He wondered what it had been thinking.

"The gang of resistance fighters knew that if they could stop the trains, the invasion would be lamed and halted," the wolf went on. "Not halted forever—the enemy is like a stream, it runs and runs, and a rock thrown into a stream might disturb the water but it won't stop the current—but halted long enough to teach their enemy that a small pack can give a nasty bite."

Tomas, who always had sympathy for the underdog, made fists of enthusiasm. The wolf leaned forward on its elbows, bringing its nose to the bars. Its ears flattened, and a glint of tooth showed behind the curl of black lips.

"The resistance fighters swore themselves to loyalty on pain of death. They arranged to meet in a private place where they could scheme undisturbed. They met in that place night after night, and eventually they thought of a plan. They invented code words and signals which would keep the plan a secret. Secrecy was vital: they didn't want anyone trying to stop them, or giving their plot away. And the secret held: until the night they put their idea into action, no one else in the village suspected what was to come. Yet the resistance fighters weren't the only ones who knew what would happen, and how, and when. *We* knew it too."

"Can you guess how we knew?" asked the llama. "Take a guess how we knew."

"The birds!" Tomas burst out triumphantly.

The wolf cocked its head; the chamois sneered aloud. "*Birds,* he says! Imagine!"

"Birds don't know what happens at night," said the llama. "Owls do, of course, but owls don't gossip. They mind their own business, owls. They look at you with those big scary eyes and they don't care what —"

The wolf interrupted, "It wasn't because of birds. It was because of Alice."

"Alice," whispered the kangaroo — and the word fluttered around the zoo like an autumn leaf across an unmown field, *Alice Alice Alice Alice,* skipping and flitting and gliding and diving as if the animals were reverently repeating the word in their heads and the zoo was indeed somewhere holy, a place where thoughts could be heard.

THE FIGHTER

She was born unexpectedly, in a garden in spring, surrounded by clouds and worms and butterflies, entering the world mere minutes before her mother left it without ever having held her child in her arms.

In the weeks that followed, many people reached out, willing to take the bewildered baby from the embrace of her grief-stricken father. The village felt keenly the loss of the young woman, who had been such a joy and an ornament. Everyone longed to ease the burden of the widower, whose family had lived in the hamlet for centuries. The father accepted the village's sympathy, and was grateful for the dishes brought to his door. But despite the advice of concerned souls he held tight to his new-born daughter, and would not send her into the care of a nurse. The baby was all he had left of his wife, and he wouldn't be parted from this remnant. More importantly, he was not a man who was made bitter by fate. He had spent all his life watching animals, and had learned from them to live with grace. There was grace in accepting death when it came, even if it seemed to come too early, and too cruelly. Accepting death meant cherishing what remained of life. And the baby girl was a small arm-ful of life, and her father kept her near as a reminder that everything that dies also lives on.

He named her Alice.

She grew up motherless but she hardly knew it, for she had a hundred mothers in the village: women who pushed her stroller when she was small, kissed her bruised knees when she was a toddler, sewed her dresses when she was old enough to go to school. She had many friends among the children of the village, for she was bold and quick-witted and talkative, and she had the talent for roguishness that most children find admirable. Her father let her run wild, that is true. He thought his daughter had lost enough, and that she shouldn't lose freedom as well. She was often punished for her rascally ways, but she took her whippings as a proud child does, as the inevitable conclusion to a fine adventure. She was clever in school, which made the teachers like her, but also lazy, which made her their frustration. She knew all the dogs and cats in the village, and every shop owner as well, and could often be found slouched against a counter, regaling the storekeeper with her ideas and opinions. She knew every corner and crook of the streets, the shortcuts and the scenic routes across town, the vantage points of rooftops and spires. She knew the farms that surrounded the village, who lived where and what crops they grew. She knew the rocky land that lay beyond the farms, and would race her bicycle on open roads and wander far along the train tracks that threaded through the hills, discovering all that could be discovered of the world in a single day. There would come a time, Alice knew, when she would find out what lay beyond a day's bicycle ride. There were other towns in this country, other countries beyond its borders, and oceans beyond them. The world belonged to and was waiting for her. But for now she belonged to her father and to her village, for there were few in the hamlet who did not think of her as their daughter too. Under their protection, she was growing up fast. "There's our Alice," people would remark as she sauntered by, already tall and beautiful, as her mother had been, her fingernails chipped and blackened, as her father's often were. "How's our Alice today?"

And of all the places she loved in her small,

cobbled version of the world, Alice's favorite place was her zoo. *Her* zoo, for it had been built by her great-grandfather and passed down to her father, and one day it would be owned by Alice herself. Of course, she had to share it: every day the wrought-iron gate was opened to the public, who dropped a brown coin into a tin in exchange for the chance to stare at, and be stared at by, a beast. Alice knew the zoo needed the money the visitors brought, but she didn't like the visitors. They were noisy and, she gradually realized, idiotic. They talked too loudly, made absurd remarks. Alice preferred it when the zoo was empty but for herself and her animals and her father. Every morning before school she walked the circle of cages, murmuring private messages to the creatures behind the bars, passing little treats to them, touching them if they stood within reach. The sight and sound of her was familiar and peaceful, and the animals liked her. Some of them were almost her pets, having arrived at the zoo as infants and been raised in the kitchen of Alice's home until they were strong enough to live in the zoo.

As Alice grew older, so too did the animals. The years brought things new and wonderful to her; for the animals it bore no such gifts. No challenges or adventures unfurled their horizons for them. The jaguar, the gibbon, the wildcat, the deer: all these woke each morning, as Alice did, and likewise went to sleep each night, but time gave them only old age and eventual death. The badger she'd adored as a toddler turned gray by her tenth birthday, and passed away. The peacock was discovered one evening lying in a puddle of its own glorious feathers. Alice was fourteen when the jaguar died, having lived all its life in the zoo. It had hated the cold weather, and feared the visitors. Its coat had been so black as to be blue. She had never seen her reflection in the creature's copper eyes. Its gaze had always looked beyond her, searching for the jungle. As she stood in a snowy field helping her father dig the cat's grave, Alice hoped that death had freed the jaguar, that maybe it was climbing vine-twisted trees now, or lapping up the warm waters of a river. She hoped so; she wept.

The jaguar was replaced by a young lion, for the zoo needed a large cat to draw in the visitors. The lion was a magnificent beast, its roars shook the entire village, and Alice loved it dearly, as she continued to love all the animals: but she found herself thinking that the zoo was not the marvelous place she'd always believed it to be. She detested the visitors who talked so brassily, who laughed at the animals and poked fingers at them. She despised the visitors' ignorance of the nature of living things. More painfully, she came to feel it was wrong to keep living creatures in cages. "This is hell for them!" she cried. "I hate this zoo! I'm ashamed of it!"

She knew how these words would wound her father, he who had devoted his life to the zoo and who loved the animals, and kept them in the best condition he could. Part of Alice wondered if she'd said these things as much to hurt her father as to defend her animals. She knew that all young creatures go through a stage when they are harshly opinionated and emotional, and perhaps she had reached this stage herself. If she were an animal, this was the age when she would turn her back on her parent and her home, and strike out to make her own future. Alice wasn't going anywhere, she was still hardly more than a child; but she wondered if something inside her wasn't already leaving her old life behind.

She remained an outgoing, lighthearted girl, but in the next few years Alice began to narrow her circle of friends, to spend more time by herself, and to lose herself often in contemplations. She continued to visit the zoo each morning and evening when the gate was closed to the public and she could be alone with the animals, stroking them, talking to them. She read about the lands they had come from and the lives they might have lived, and told them stories about themselves using all the facts she'd learned. In the gloaming light the animals heard words like *shore, mountain, gale, glacier, blood, lair, cub.* She put her hand between the bars and ran her palm over the chamois's coat. Her fingernails left five tracks in the smooth dense hair. "I would free you if I could," she told the beasts that lay listening to her. She did not tell them what else she knew, something she'd known all along, a fact she'd heard her father state a hundred, a thousand times. Freed and returned to their original habitat, the zoo animals would not survive. Some had been born in captivity, and knew no other world. Some had been taken as newborns from their dens, before they'd learned the ways of the wilderness. Some had been found injured and brought to the sanctuary of the zoo, but carried echoes of that injury still. None of them, whatever their history, would be able to survive without bars.

And then life changed for everyone in Alice's world, though least noticeably for the zoo's animals. The invasion came.

At first it seemed like a story or a joke. In the village, everything they heard was conflicting and confused: some said the invaders were seizing the nation, some insisted the invaders were only passing through. Some believed the invasion would solve the nation's problems, protect it, strengthen it, purify it of all that was undesirable; to others, the invasion meant doom to the nation, it was the very worst thing that could happen. Whatever the truth, it very quickly became clear that the invaders, having arrived, did not intend to leave. They were claiming the nation, and meant to claim others. The invading soldiers came like oil out of the ground and flowed everywhere, and the flow could not be stopped.

The nation was poor, and weak compared to the invaders. It stood no chance of driving back such a massive army. There were those who would not have driven it out even if they were able. They wanted the security that the invaders seemed to promise. But there were many, many others who were outraged that the invaders were stealing and debasing their homeland in this callous, lawless way.

Alice and her father were among these many. Alice was infuriated, and burned to retaliate. Her father was more prudent, saying, "The important thing is to keep ourselves safe." Alice, who was nineteen years old, believed her father a coward. She wanted to fight. And as the months wore by, she heard stories of people who were indeed taking the battle against the enemy into their own hands. Alice decided to do the same. She gathered together her closest friends and said, "This country is ours. It doesn't belong to the invaders. We can't stop them, but we can hurt them. We *must*."

Her friends agreed without hesitation, for they too were young and bold. They needed a plan, and a private place to make it. "The zoo," said Alice. "No one goes there at night. I have a key to the gate. We can meet in the zoo."

And so the friends became conspirators. There were seven of them. They convened in the zoo each midnight, and sat on the grass and on the green bench scheming while the village slept and the animals lay quietly listening, their ears tilting to catch every word. The wolf licked its teeth, the bear sighed troubledly, the chamois shook its horned head. The conspirators proposed, argued, agreed, disagreed. When they'd finally settled on their plan, they celebrated by passing around a bottle of wine. The animals watched them drink from it, laughing and buoyant, ruby drops falling from their chins. The resistance fighters looked like children at that moment, children playing at a grown-up game.

They chose the night of their attack with care, having studied the railway timetable and discovered which trains were important to the enemy and which they could ignore. They did not want to hurt anyone, so they made sure to target only the cargo trains. As the chosen night approached, the fighters grew edgy and excited. In the darkness they acted out their plan to the animals, testing it for flaws, rehearsing their individual roles. The llama watched with shining eyes, grinding its teeth in thought.

The night, when it came, was a black one, the moon a thin cat's claw. As a child, Alice had made many hidey-holes in ditches and rock piles: now the resistance fighters took from these hiding places the explosives and timber they'd stashed there. Working in darkness and silence, they laid the explosives between the train tracks. A little farther

down the track they built a pyre across the sleep-
ers. Then they stepped into the blackness to wait.

In the still of night they could hear the locomotive coming from a long distance away. Its wheels
shrilled, its engine huffed. The conspirators gripped
each other's hands. The timing of everything had
to be perfect. Alice's heart thumped hard.

When the train disappeared behind a certain
hill, the fighters lit the pyre. The timber had been
doused in kerosene, so it caught fast and blazed
lustily. When the train chugged round the near side
of the hill, it found its route blocked by a tower of
flame.

The driver slowed the locomotive with much
shifting of levers and shrieking of wheels, and
brought it to a stop. The driver was a fellow country-
man, not one of the invaders. Alice yelled at the top
of her voice, "Jump, man! Get away!"

And the driver understood what was about to
happen. He leapt from the engine room just as
the explosives were triggered beneath the train. A
mighty roar and an eruption of white light threw

Alice and her friends off their feet. They opened their eyes to see the train on fire and howling like a monster that has crawled up from the boiling core of the earth and exists only in the worst nightmares. Flames lashed from its windows, flashed between the wheels, flapped from the roof like red dragon wings.

Safe in their cages inside the zoo, the animals flinched.

The resistance fighters gathered their feet and rushed back to the village. Each went their separate way through the streets, returning like innocents to their beds. None was able to sleep, however. The thrill had been too great. They couldn't erase from their heads the image of the burning train. They couldn't stop hearing the almighty *boom* of the explosion, or forget the force of its heat. Everything had gone as planned; everything had gone more than right.

Outside, the church bell was tolling, and flashlight beams went bobbing over the cobbles as the villagers, startled from slumber, hurried out to investigate the commotion. The flames were higher and hungrier now, feeding on the timberwork of the carriages, the wooden crates of cargo. The driver was roaming the tracks half-stupefied, babbling something that no one could understand — eventually he was carted away. There was nothing that could be done to save the train, and no lives or property seemed to be endangered, so the townspeople stood about in their pajamas watching the monster burn. The flames painted their faces orange, and blackened the grass all around. Youngsters in the crowd thought they'd never see anything more exciting. Nobody was afraid.

But by the morning it was widely understood what the addled driver had been trying to say. Resistance fighters had blown up the train, which was all very well and good . . . except that traveling on the train had been an important man, and this man was important not because he was clever or rich or cunning, but because he was a much-loved friend of the invaders' leader.

Alice heard this news when she came down for

breakfast. She sat at the table staring blankly at the buttered toast her father had put on her plate. She had not known that this man, the Leader's friend, would be on the train. According to her research, nothing but uniforms and metal for making ammunition was supposed to be on the train. She felt her victory sliding away. She felt the dreadfulness of what she'd done. She felt peril rise before her like a tidal wave.

The leader of the invasion would be furious about losing the locomotive and its cargo, and the destruction of the tracks. The resistance fighters had expected this to be so. But to lose his dear friend was a different thing altogether, something that would cut into the Leader's notoriously passionate heart. He would certainly retaliate against those who had done this thing: and the vengeance of such a ruthless man was an awful thing to contemplate.

Alice saw clearly not only the jeopardy she was in, but the danger she had brought down on her village. She realized too that, although she was almost grown, she still had much to learn. She pushed away the toast and said, "Tata," a word she hadn't used since childhood. "Tata, I have something to tell you. It was I who blew up the train."

She told her father the story of the resistance fighters. Her father, drained and speechless, seemed to listen. She never knew that he was listening most closely to a voice inside his head. *You have lost her,* the voice was saying. *This is the last you'll see of her.*

At the conclusion of her story, the father told his daughter the only thing he could say. His heart was being broken to pieces, but his voice was calm and even. "Leave this place quickly," he said. "Get as far from here as you can. Go up into the mountains. I'm told there are resistance fighters hiding there. You'll be safer with them. You aren't safe here, Alice. The Leader will be looking for you. And maybe other people will look for you too. People who are our neighbors, people who are angry and fearful . . ."

Alice understood what her father was saying, but she set her mouth in exactly the way her beautiful mother used to do. "Tata, no. I don't want to. I should stay, and face up to what I've done. I have killed a man. I have put the village in peril. Only a coward runs away."

Her father clutched his head and cried, "Don't argue with me, Alice! For once, do as you are told! Remember that your life is precious—if not to you, then to me! Make clever decisions, not foolish ones! Be brave when you *have* to be, not when it merely seems noble! Go to the mountains. Find friends there. Keep fighting the enemy. Fight and fight. Fight with every ounce of your courage. I'll be proud of you, if you do that. I won't be proud if you simply sit here until they come to drag you away!"

Alice stared. She knew she must go. But her heart tightened with grief, and her eyes filled with tears. "Come with me then, Tata," she begged. "I don't want to leave you."

"I can't," her father answered. "I must stay with the zoo. The animals need me." And this was a truth Alice recognized, she who had been raised alongside the animals and knew better than anyone how deeply they needed somebody to care about them. There was no time to lose—dawn had already given way to day, and news of the train wreck was riding the breeze to reach the ears of the Leader—but while her father packed her bag Alice shielded her face with a cloak and ran through streets she'd known all her life, through a neighborhood that had seen her grow from a child to a woman, through a town that was her center of the world; and went to the zoo.

She walked the perimeter of the cages, skimming her fingers along the bars. She whispered to the creatures that lived behind them, as well as to the ones who had once been and were gone and lived only in her memory. Her life would be different from now on, frightening and exhilarating, reticent and precarious, and Alice felt ready to face it only because she'd lived beside animals who longed for such fierce existences. Time was ticking, and she needed to hurry. Reaching the pebbled path beside the eagle's cage, she turned for a final look. The kangaroo was watching her, trembling in the cold. There was no minute to spare for running her hand over its scratchy gray face. "I have to leave." Alice spoke to all of them. "But I'll come back to you, I promise. Tata will stay, and care for you while I'm gone. But I will come back."

THE GIFT

"*And has she come back?*" asked Tomas.

"She has not," replied the wolf. "The moon has grown big and small and big again, but she hasn't returned."

"Lovely Alice," sighed the llama. "Everything is wrong since Alice went away."

"Where has she gone?" puzzled the kangaroo.

"She's forgotten us," said the unhappy bear.

"She hasn't forgotten us!" bleated the chamois. "She was *our* daughter too! She was the daughter of the zoo. She won't forget us. She'll come back as soon as she can."

"She promised she would," said the llama, "and she will."

And Andrej heard it again then, *Alice Alice Alice*, like a leaf skittering on the wind. He was well acquainted with the kind of mountains into which the girl had fled. He wondered what she, someone accustomed to comfort, would make of the rugged ground, the chalk-white stone, the trees that were stern and ungiving. He thought of his uncle Marin, who had taught Andrej the tricks of surviving in those harsh ranges. Alice would need the help of somebody like Marin, who knew about fire and shelter. Andrej tried to hear if *Marin Marin Marin* was wafting around him like a leaf: but the wolf had risen and was speaking again, and Andrej looked up to listen.

"The morning after Alice went away, the village Mayor came to the zoo. He cast a wide shadow and smelled of fat and hide. He stood on the grass where you two pups are sitting now. He talked to the zoo's owner. He said, *I have learned a lot in the past night and day, Mikael. I know that your daughter, Alice, concocted the plan to destroy the train. I'm sure she meant well, as children in their escapades always do. But what she did has made the village look bad in the eyes of the Leader, and that's an unfortunate way to look, don't you agree? A vulnerable way to look, Mikael. We must do something to prove to the Leader that we regret what happened to his dear good friend, and that we sympathize with his loss. A gift to illustrate our apologies. Something to assure him we'll behave ourselves from now on.*"

The bear gave a groan, the sound of a log toppling in a fireplace. The llama too was bothered, lifting its feet fretfully. "I don't like this story," it whimpered.

"Be quiet!" barked the chamois. "Let it be told!"

"Alice," piped the kangaroo.

The wolf ignored them, its oak-colored eyes on the children. "The zoo's owner thought that a gift was a good idea, but he asked the Mayor, *What can we do? We're only a humble village. We don't have anything that might console a man like our enemy's leader — a man who wants nothing less than to own the entire world.*"

The lioness's tail gave a sudden violent lashing, like an asp lunging out of a basket. "Wolf!" growled the bear, and the llama balked skittishly and made a frightened noise. The wolf glanced up, hesitating for a heartbeat before carrying on with the story. "The Mayor smiled at the zoo's owner and replied, *No, Mikael, that's where you are wrong. We have something rare and precious of which our enemy's leader is very fond. Apparently he likes animals, dogs and pigeons and horses, and of course all magnificent and exotic wild things. I don't suppose a man as preoccupied as the Leader has time for visiting zoos, however — do you? So maybe we should send a piece of our zoo to him. Make the Leader a gift of your finest* beasts, Mikael, and hopefully his fury will be soothed. And maybe, in doing so, you can make some small amends for the danger that your daughter has brought to our door."

"Oh no." Tomas looked around for help. "No, that's not fair . . ."

"Not fair!" The wolf was amused. "The zoo's owner thought so too. He bristled like a terrier. A terrier with no teeth and no bark. He said nothing."

"What could he say?" snarled the bear. "What choice did he have?"

"Tell the story!" screamed the chamois.

The wolf flexed its claws against the stone. "The zoo's owner said nothing. Perhaps because there was nothing to say. A cage door was opened, and something was done to console the Leader."

"Something terrible was done," whispered the llama.

The kangaroo echoed, in its odd static voice, "Something terrible was done."

"Was it the boar's cage that was opened?" asked

Andrej, for they'd seen and heard nothing of that animal and it was starting to seem ominous, the square of shifting blackness labeled KANEC, from which no sound escaped. "Did the boar go to the Leader?"

"The boar?" The wolf snorted. "Do you really think a *pig* would impress the commander of a great ocean of army? No, it wasn't the boar. They opened up the lions' cage and brought out the lion and the three infant cubs."

The brothers stared into the moonlit haze, seeing the wolf's words take the shape of a key in a padlock, a lion on a leash, cubs clawing and wriggling to be freed. Their gaze slid to the lioness, who had not risen from the ground. Whose tail lay lank and seemed hardly alive. "That terrible thing," murmured the kangaroo.

"That afternoon, the lion and his mewling cubs were coaxed into wooden crates; and the crates were loaded onto a truck; and the truck was driven away. We have not seen them since. The zoo's owner traveled in the truck with the lions, to tend them during their journey. He gave us food and water before he went, enough for several days. We believe he meant to return—Alice told us he was staying here, to take care of the zoo. But the moon has bloomed and died and bloomed again, and he hasn't returned in all that time: we haven't seen him since."

No one said anything. In its dark and shielded corner, the eagle shook its wings. Eventually Andrej said, "But the village is destroyed."

"That is so."

"Why? If the Leader has the lions, why is the village destroyed?"

The wolf blinked languidly, settling down on thin haunches. "A lion and three cubs couldn't console the Leader any more than a boar could, that's why. The Mayor was a fool to imagine they would. A whole pride of lions couldn't have done so. Only revenge could do that thing. Revenge, and the teaching of a lesson to any other village that was thinking about resisting the invasion. The first bomb fell the morning after the lions went away. Another and another bomb, and more after that, until the village was in pieces, and all the people gone. Since that time, the village has been silent. I don't think even a mouse lives there now. Nothing remains but dust and stone and this story. Even so, the invaders drop more bombs sometimes, to make sure the rubble is repentant too."

The brothers plucked the ashy tips of the grass while they thought over all they'd heard: over the disastrous attack on the cargo train and the loss of the zoo's daughter, Alice; over the disappearance of the lions and the owner of the zoo; over the unforgiving bombings that had destroyed the village and cast out its blameless people. They thought of the weeks that the animals had spent trapped in their cages, surviving on rain and dew and whatever moths and petals and scraps of weed happened to blow in through the bars. "Everyone is gone." Tomas examined the facts, a frown printing creases on his brow. "Everything is ended, and everyone is gone, except for the animals in the zoo. You're still here, because you can't leave. And nobody stayed behind to care about you."

"That is so," the wolf replied.

THE MEAL

Andrej's heart felt unbearably heavy. He looked at
his small grimy brother, whose hair fell in his face
and who needed a bath and a new set of clothes;
he looked at the lioness, whose massive chiseled

head rested leadenly on her paws. Wilma, on the bench, was making no noise, and even the wolf seemed finally quietened. "We have some food," Andrej heard himself say. "There won't be much to go around, but it's better than nothing."

Tomas caught his breath, delighted. The animals stood to watch as he upended Andrej's pack across the lawn. Into the grass tumbled their treasures — a torn comic, a set of playing cards, a blue cap, a brass bullet, a pair of aviator goggles with a stretched and broken head strap. Out fell candles and cutlery and a can opener, matches, a flashlight, and the corkscrew Andrej had found in the village. Out clattered plates and bowls and dented mugs made of tin. Out came their money, secreted like a sardine; out came all the tradable goods Andrej had taken from the caravans — carving tools and razor blades, jewelry in silver and leather — which always made Tomas's chest hurt to see. Out bounced a rock of cheese and a bruised apple, and two dinner rolls speckled with mold. Out dropped a chunk of liverwurst and an almost-complete packet of biscuits.

Out rolled Wilma's priceless pot of lemon butter, and a matching but full pot of jam. Tomas stood all these aside, shook the bag and peered inside it, and plunged in an investigating arm. From the bottom of the pack he drew the prize of their scavengings, a fragrant lump wrapped in a tea towel: for an instant he hesitated, and glanced at Andrej, who, though he knew how it would feel the next day when there was nothing to eat, nodded and said, "That too." So Tomas set the lump on the ground and unwrapped the tea towel to reveal a chewed ham bone, the smell of which made the wolf groan. The assembled food appeared a scanty feast for the voracious inhabitants of a zoo, yet Tomas sat back smiling, bountiful and proud.

"I will have the apple," the llama decided.

"Jam!" The monkey yelled as if volted. "Jam, jam!"

"I am partial to lichen," announced the chamois, "but of course one is willing to eat bread."

Andrej looked over his shoulder at the bear, who lay so heaped and dejected. "What would you like?"

"Nothing." The bear closed its eyes. "Not hungry."

"Good!" said the llama. "More for us."

"Pointless anyway," the chamois said shortly. "A bear has a tremendous appetite. They can eat until their stomachs drag on the ground. A bit of biscuit would be like a snowflake on a mountain, to a bear."

The wolf cocked its ears. "You *must* be hungry. If you were out in the forest, you'd be fattening up for winter. You'd be hungry enough to eat an elk."

"Or a chamois," hissed the monkey.

The chamois clattered to the front of its pen and bawled, "I've warned you before, you ridiculous *chimp!* There is nothing amusing about saying such things! We are all in this together! We're *all* hungry, we're *all* thirsty, we're all locked behind the same bars! This is neither the place nor the time for jokes about eating each other! It's *not* clever. It changes *nothing.* And it's utterly disrespectful to my feelings! It's uncalled for, do you understand?"

The wolf said, "You're only saying that because you're so edible."

The monkey sprang through the ropes and turned somersaults, screeching with amusement. Infuriated, the chamois lowered its head and charged. Its hooked horns struck the iron bars with a *gong* that reverberated hugely against the still air; immediately it reared back, fixed its target, and attacked the bars again. The eagle, alarmed, launched from its perch and flung clumsily around its pen, screaming metallically. The lioness joined in with chuffing roars. The wolf, sprinting the length of its cage, let out several excited yips before raising its white chin to howl.

The din was chaotic. Wilma, woken in confusion, took a huge breath and contributed to the pandemonium some bloodcurdling shrieks of her own. Tomas clamped his hands to his ears and yelled, "What's happening?"

"The food has sent them mad!" shouted the llama. "They are uncivilized!"

The ruckus was so horrendous that Tomas imagined the pilots in the three long-gone airplanes hearing the uproar and flying back to investigate.

Quickly he scooped the bread, jam and liverwurst into his shirtfront and scuttled across the grass. Twisting the lid from the jam, he offered the jar to the monkey, who abruptly stopped screeching, snatched the condiment through the bars, and leapt away with it into a corner. Spinning on his heels Tomas ran back over the grass, past the bench and the marble mermaid to the chamois's pen. He bowled the bread rolls between the bars and the chamois danced backward as the food bopped toward it, eyes boggling and heavy horns brandished. Tomas approached the wolf's cage more tentatively, proffering the liverwurst. "Don't bite me," he begged, reaching hastily into the cage. The wolf cut short its howl and glared at him, but did not dart forward to bite. Their choir silenced, the eagle and lioness fell mute; the lioness padded listlessly to the rear of her enclosure, and the eagle shrugged shut its great wings.

Which left only the sound of Wilma, wailing anxiously. Andrej picked her up and found her bottle and tried to interest her in the creamy dregs, but his effort to distract her seemed only to further offend: threads of milk ran untasted across her tongue as she roared out her fear and upset. The bear watched her arch in her brother's arms and kick against the bonds of the shawl, her face a knot of scorched flesh. For the first time all night it raised itself up on its lumberlike legs, a fog of brown hairs drifting from it, its paws making a rough sound on the stone. Its solemn gaze roved its restive companions before returning to Andrej. "Forgive them," it sighed. "They sit here every day with nothing to do and nothing to see. Their minds are getting misty. Soon they'll all be as lost as the seal."

Andrej put his squalling sister on his shoulder and walked around joggling her. The big moon was still shining above them, radiating its sugary light onto the earth. Perhaps the only corner where its white beams didn't reach was inside the wild boar's enclosure. Andrej turned away from that maw of blackness, and carried Wilma across to the seal's cage.

The shiny streak of animal was sweeping up

and down the length of its pool exactly as it had been doing when the children first saw it. Its pace, which was swift, was also unaltering, nor did its ceaseless circuit veer even slightly from its invisible track. Somehow it was propelling itself through the water, although Andrej saw no movement of flipper or tail. The seal seemed nothing more than a shadowy shape that had taken on a relentless life and a strange, perpetual mission. Over Wilma's sobbing Andrej asked the bear, "Is this all it does? Just swim back and forth?"

"What else should it do?" said the bear.

Patting the baby between her small shoulders, Andrej watched the sea creature flip and glide. Its seamless looping was hypnotic. The ripples it made on the greasy surface of the water were perfectly identical and flawlessly rhythmical, like the beat of an army drum. They lapped the stone edges of the pool and fell back with the most meager splash. The longer Andrej's gaze followed the animal up and down the pool, the more forcefully he felt the creature's trapped misery. "Poor thing," he said.

"They should have left it in the ocean. In the ocean, it would never have bumped into a wall."

"It has never swum in the ocean," the bear replied. "Somewhere far away there's a place where the rocks are frozen and sprinkled with snow and the ocean beats the rocks as if it's trying to crack them like coconuts—I'm not saying this place exists, this is only what I've heard; I'm telling you the story as I heard the zoo's owner tell it, so don't ask me to explain—and that's where the seal was born. When it wasn't much older than that cub in your arms, a boatload of fishermen came to the shore where the seal pup was sleeping beside its mother. The fishermen were hungry, so they ate the seal's mother. I've never eaten seal meat but I imagine it's salty. Salty, and without bones. They should have finished off the young one too, but it had soft eyes and a fluffy trusting face, and they couldn't bring themselves to do it . . . but it was a motherless infant now, and out of kindness they couldn't leave it to suffer. Instead of killing it, they decided to make money from it. I'm not surprised, I've seen how much humans love money, how they snuffle around squawking in the grass when they drop the tiniest coin. Anyway, the fishermen took the pup in the boat with them, and whenever they arrived at a port they charged women and children a few coins to pet it."

Wilma's cries were simmering down; Andrej cuddled and cooed to her while he contemplated the seal. He had visited countless circuses and sideshows with their garish tents, frisky ponies, cracking whips, shouting spruikers. It wouldn't have been like that for the seal: he saw dingy corners of pubs and piers, babbling voices, grabbing hands.

"Nothing alive stays an infant forever," continued the bear. "Some behave as if they have, but the fact is that they haven't, and they should take a good hard look at themselves. Soon the pup was growing. The fishermen taught it tricks—to beg, to balance a ball, to bark on command—but it was always hungry and needing attention, and eventually the fishermen decided they liked living without their pet more than living with it. Trained and tamed as it was, it would have been a waste to eat it; so they sold it to a man who said he had use for a seal, and this man lost it in a bet to another, who gave it to a man who planned to make a name for himself by writing the world's longest book about seals, who lost it when all his worldly possessions were taken by the debt collector, for whom everything has a price. The debt collector spread the word that he had a seal for sale. And because the penguin who'd been living in that pool had grown huge and died after gorging on pastries and boiled sweets all its life, the owner of the zoo bought the seal to fill the empty cage, and put a sign on the bars saying *Don't feed the seal.*"

Andrej rocked his sister, watching the seal swim. When its whiskery snout unexpectedly broke the surface he nearly cried out, thinking it meant to leap onto land. Instead it took a wheezy breath and resumed its flight back and forth. Its ceaseless glide to nowhere was a piteous thing to witness. Andrej had never seen a living being so stifled, so pointlessly driven. "Do you think it remembers the ocean?"

It would hurt less if it had forgotten, but the bear replied, "Of course it remembers. Its mind is filled with the crashing of waves. The ocean called out to it from the moment it was born. Its ancestors swam there; its kin swim there today. It remembers the ocean because its blood and bones cannot forget it. Somewhere out there, there's a gap in the water, a place which is hollow because the seal isn't there."

Andrej thought about it — the notion that the world was riddled with holes where certain people and animals were meant to be, but weren't. "I've never seen the ocean," he mused. "I don't know what it looks like. Do you?"

"No I do not," the bear admitted.

Andrej nodded. Uncle Marin would have known. He rested his cheek atop Wilma's warm head. "Is there a gap in the mountains somewhere?" he asked.

"Of course," the bear replied. "I'm not there."

Andrej considered the great brown beast slouched behind the bars, its broad stump of grizzly muzzle and its long warlock claws. The stone had flattened the bear's coat smooth in places so the hair lay against its body like rich soil. "How did you come here?" he asked.

The bear drew a breath and heaved it out as a sigh. "You can't catch a grown bear and put it in a cage. You can only take a cub from a den. But before you do that, you must deal with the cub's mother, who'll fight to protect her infant without any care for her own life."

Andrej said nothing. He remembered the last words he'd heard his own mother speak: *Run, children.* And he had done as she'd commanded, and run. He had run with the memory of his mother standing straight and tall, her dark hair riding the breeze as she'd turned to look for him. When, hours later, he had crept through the trees, the clearing where he'd last seen her was empty but for the burned-out shells of caravans, and boot prints where soldiers had been.

THE LAW

Tomas, meanwhile, had returned to the cache of
food, piling into the hammock of his shirtfront the
biscuits, apple and cheese. The llama, which was

quite tame, had lifted the apple out of his palm and crunched it wetly with peg teeth. Tomas didn't know what a kangaroo ate, and the marsupial didn't seem to know either; so the boy had broken some biscuits and scattered them inside the cage, and the kangaroo, after much timid sniffing, hopped forward to nibble at the shards. "Funny little creature," Tomas whispered; privately, he liked the kangaroo best. He came to the bear's cage now, and reached between the bars to place the cheese on the stone floor. "You might be hungry later," he said. Sidling close to his brother, he muttered, "What does an eagle eat, Andrej?"

"Bunnies," said the wolf, licking liverwurst from its chops.

"Baby chamois!" said the monkey, its face rosy with raspberry jam.

Andrej said, "Why don't you ask the eagle?"

"It won't answer," warned the bear.

"Why not?" Tomas frowned. "Can't it speak?"

"It's not that it can't, only that it won't. No bird in a cage ever speaks. What is there to say? The sky is everywhere, churning above its head, blue and endless, calling out to it. But the caged bird can't answer anything except *I cannot*. And those words are so painful to its feathery spirit that a caged bird prefers to say nothing."

The llama was cleaning its face with a fastidious tongue; pausing in its ablutions it said, "That eagle has been in that cage since the day it hatched from an egg. I remember when it was hardly bigger than a mouse, the ugly tiny thing; the zoo's owner used to feed it mashed lizard from a spoon. It's never flown through the sky, that eagle, never once in its life. Yet it broods and mopes over something that's never been. It is a very silly bird."

The bear didn't comment, only raised its eyes to the night. Andrej followed its gaze into the sky. "Can you see it?" asked the bear.

"I can," said Andrej: an empty place amongst the stars, where the eagle should have been.

"I thank you for the cheese," said the bear.

Andrej told his brother, "Give the eagle some pieces of ham."

"And what about the seal?"

"Don't worry about that seal." The wolf had lain down to groom its legs and didn't look up from the work. "That seal isn't hungry. It doesn't think about food. It thinks about nothing except the empty hole in the sea."

"It wants to fill its place!" yapped the monkey.

"Alice," breathed the kangaroo.

Wilma whined, and Andrej stroked her head. He looked at the circle of cages and at the inmates inside them. He thought of the life he had lived with his family in the caravan, roaming wherever they'd wanted to go. "The whole world is your home, Andrej," his father had told him. "We Rom are not like the *gadje*, these people you see building houses and hoeing fields and fencing off what they claim is theirs. We Rom are closer to the animals than to people like that. Unburdened, unowned, and free." It was something to be proud of, the state of being free. It was something animals had that humans envied and respected. And yet . . . these zoo animals weren't free. Dust was more free than they were.

The gnats that landed on the surface of the water had more liberty than the seal that swam through it. The iron bars stole away from them the one great gift they were born to have. In sudden frustration and anguish Andrej said, "It's not right to take a bear from the mountains or an eagle from the sky or a monkey from the jungle or a seal from the sea. It's not *right* to lock you in cages where there's no grass or rivers or trees. It's a *terrible* thing to do. The owner of this zoo must be a *wicked* man!"

The llama gasped. "Don't say that! The owner is good! When the owner was here, we weren't hungry. We weren't lonely. I wasn't confused. There were no bombs dropping out of rumble-things. All those bad things only started happening *after* he went away. So he must be a good man, you see? You see, you stupid child?"

"The owner is not a wicked man," the bear agreed. "He is just a man, with the peculiar ways of man. You are a mysterious animal, you know. A bear does what a bear must do to keep itself alive. But a man does many things that he has no need to do."

Andrej thought about the day the soldiers found the caravans in the clearing and admitted, "Yes, that's true." He looked into the moonlight that lay everywhere over the zoo, wishing he had water to give the animals or something more to feed them, wishing he had . . . *the keys.* One cage was still cloaked in deathly dark and silence, a silence that was lurking, a darkness like the edge of a disquieting dream. "What about the boar?" he asked. "Is it hungry? Will it eat biscuits? Is it even inside that pen? Or has it gone to fill an empty place in the forest?"

"Who knows?" said the chamois. "Who knows anything about that boar?"

"That boar is mysterious, as men are," said the bear.

"Find out!" said the monkey. "Put a hand in the cage—find out!"

The wolf lifted its nose. "I can smell that little pig. His tusks are close—"

"Find out!" the monkey goaded deliriously.

"—but he has been silent for a long time, since

before the bombs began to fall—almost as if he knew the bombs were coming, and didn't want to spoil the surprise. That would be typical of him."

"Typical of him to find a way out of his cage," added the chamois, "but to keep it a secret like a trove of buried acorns. An unpleasant and petty little hog, that one."

"He was *charming* as a piglet," said the llama. "Remember how darling? But he grew into a bore. Furious and furious and furiouser, always sniffling and snuffling and tearing at the bars."

"One wouldn't be surprised if he'd chewed his way through them," concluded the chamois. "He's always in such a frenzy."

The brothers gazed dubiously into the blackness that crouched inside the boar's cage. Andrej remembered what Marin had told him about wild pigs, how cunning they could be, how treacherous their tusks. The tusks could cut a hunting dog to pieces, or open a man's thigh to the bone. Andrej closed his eyes and concentrated. Marin had said pigs were clever and vicious, but would he have agreed they were smart enough to escape a locked cage, fierce enough to cut through iron? *Marin*, he thought: *Marin*. Opening his eyes, Andrej said sternly, "You're teasing us."

The animals did not reply. The chamois flicked its bob of tail, the llama smacked its lips. The wolf craned forward to sniff the stone where the liver-wurst had been. "Where—where—where would it be?" asked Tomas with a splutter. "If the boar has escaped, where will he be?"

"*Out* of his cage," said the llama.

"That boar likes bombs," said the kangaroo.

"And *hates* everything else," said the chamois.

"Especially boys," said the wolf.

"It *hasn't* escaped." Andrej raised his chin. "It couldn't have escaped. If it was in its cage when the zoo's owner left, and no one has opened the cage since then, then it *must* be in its cage. They're teasing us, Tom."

"Yes, teasing." Tomas smiled tepidly.

"Give the boar the rest of the biscuits."

"Yes, he'll like biscuits," Tomas agreed. But he

tugged at his brother's sleeve and mumbled, "Come with me?"

The lioness lifted her head to watch them cross the grass. They walked beneath the branches of the maple, past the bench and the mermaid and the packs with their strewn innards. Approaching the boar's cage they saw the bars harden out of the shadows, saw the sign that said KANEC. Andrej knew that the animals were teasing, that logically the boar could not be loose: but his certainty suddenly revealed itself to have a dank side, like a branch that has lain many months in a puddle, and he paused while moonlight still touched his face, abruptly less sure. "The sign wouldn't say there was a boar in the cage if the boar wasn't in the cage," whispered Tomas, but Andrej knew this was a child's reasoning, impossible to rely upon. He knew, also, what his father and uncle would expect him to do—what all the animals were watching in expectation of him doing. He must tell Tomas to stop here, he must go forward into the darkness bravely and alone because the strong are duty-bound to protect the weak, it is a law of nature and thus of *rightness:* and in that instant Andrej understood that the soldiers and their leader were not obeying this law, and that any victory they achieved wouldn't last because nature's law would not be overthrown. He wished Alice were here so he could tell her this inevitable truth he'd unexpectedly grasped: that the invaders couldn't win the war, she didn't have to blow up a train, there was no need to leave her animals—she had only to wait for nature to right itself, as it always must and will. Bunching the baby inside the shawl he passed her into his brother's arms, and took from Tomas the biscuits in their crumpled paper bag. "Stay here, where it's light," he ordered; then lowered his head to whisper. "If something happens, you run. Don't try to help me. Hold on to Wilma, and run." And then, before Tomas could answer, he stepped forward into the blackness and walked up to the wild boar's cage.

Scanning the darkness inside the enclosure, Andrej saw nothing except shadows overlapping one another, and a few leaves that had blown between the bars. Such pitchness could conceal a troll. He listened, but heard nothing—no grunt, no scuttling of hooves. Such silence could be the last thing one ever heard. "Boar?" he said. The cage reeked potently of hog, but that didn't mean the boar was in the pen. It might be hunched at Andrej's ankles, rankled and with razor tusks. Andrej's heart thudded; *Marin*, he called, but felt only emptiness, remembered only that attempts to placate an avowed enemy usually fail, as the village had discovered when it gave away its lions. Nevertheless he stood his ground: "I've brought you some biscuits, in case you're hungry," he informed the invisible animal. His blood sang as he reached between the bars to lay the offering on the stone. His wrist looked thin and breakable at the end of his sleeve. Withdrawing his hand, he wiped crumbs from his fingers. "I hope you like them," he told the unshifting blackness. Then he backed away swiftly, but not so swiftly as to seem afraid, into the welcoming moonlight. Tomas, squeezing Wilma, hurried to his side.

"I told you!" Unscathed and standing in the

light, Andrej rode a wave of triumph. "I told you it would be all right!" He wished his father had been here to witness his courage, his mother to approve of his kindness. He was once again convinced that the boar wasn't free . . . but he had no desire to repeat the experience, and when Tomas said, "The eagle and the lioness haven't had dinner yet," he was pleased to cross the grass to where the lioness lived, where a boar might be afraid to go.

The ham heaved out a repellent odor when they peeled away the tea towel. Andrej stripped off a handful of the stringy pink meat and upended it into the eagle's cage. The big mahogany bird dropped from its perch to step boldly toward them, talons clicking on stone. Its stately head was like a butcher's hook, its wings a heavy saddle astride its body. They saw the intricate mosaic of its quills, the rich butter-yellow of its legs and beak, the vitality in its crimson eyes. "Beautiful bird, won't you talk?" Tomas asked, but the eagle would not.

Lastly they approached the lioness's cage, Tomas carrying Wilma, Andrej bearing the ham bone. The lioness rushed to the bars and swiped her paws against them, snarling impatiently. Andrej fed the bone partway through the bars, and she gripped it with her ivory teeth and yanked it into the cage. As it pulled from his hands he felt her force, the force of an avalanche or a hurricane. She consumed the ham in mere moments, her incisors carving the meat from the bone, pinning the bone between her paws and effortlessly eating that too, the bone cracking and splintering horribly. When the meal was as gone as if it had never been, she lay on the stone licking her teeth and considering the children. She gazed particularly at the baby: after much licking and gazing and considering she asked, "Is your infant warm?"

Andrej glanced at Wilma. The shawl was woolen; the night wasn't too cold. "I think so."

"She looks pale," said the lioness. "Bring her closer. Let me see."

Andrej took Wilma from Tomas's arms, came forward and held his sister up to the bars. The baby, half asleep, squirmed like a grub in the shawl.

The lioness stared; then, in a flash, she was on her feet and speeding toward the bars. Andrej snatched Wilma to him and leapt backward, but the lioness didn't seem thwarted or insulted: "That's better," she said. "Keep her near your body. She will be warmed by the heat of your blood."

Andrej's heart was hammering with shock. He could hardly find words to say. "I know that," he managed to answer. "My mother told me."

"Your mother? You remember her?"

Andrej nodded shallowly. "Yes, we remember her."

"I do not think my cubs will remember me," said the lioness, "when they are grown, as you are."

Tomas, who had shrunk behind his brother, emerged and spoke up timorously. "I'm sad that the lion and your cubs were taken away because of the war."

The lioness's eyes turned toward him. Her head was a magnificent thing, like the head of the sun. Her long willowy body was supple and strong as a river. "Because of *your* war," she said.

"It's not our war," Andrej said quickly. "It's the *gadje*'s war."

"It makes me sad," said Tomas.

The lioness's lime gaze shuttered away from him, returning to the baby. "Three Rom children rambling alone through the night," she mused. "I think you must have lost a family too."

Tomas drew a wobbly breath and said again, "I'm sad."

THE KITE

What Andrej remembered perfectly was the scarlet kite. Someone had brought it to the celebration and all afternoon it zipped and soared above the trees, although down in the clearing there was almost no breeze and the women had to flap their aprons to encourage the cooking flames to bite. Andrej played soccer with the other boys, most of whom were his cousins or in some other way related. The weather was pleasantly warm that day and the boys played without shirts, and in the rough-and-tumble their olive-skinned chests became scuffed with grass and dirt. Whenever Andrej paused to catch his breath, he looked up in search of the kite. Its canopy was cardinal-red, its tail a string of white feathers. He remembered seeing his cousin Mirabela running in circles with the kite jolting and swooping above her and a gaggle of the younger children dashing along behind her, begging to hold on to the string. Tomas was not among them, nor was he playing soccer. He could be shy with people he didn't know well, and whenever there was a gathering he preferred to stay close to his mother.

Andrej wished Uncle Marin and some of the other men would join the game. It was always more fun when the grown-ups played too. They kicked the ball cleverly, and with such focused strength; when they scored a goal, they turned cartwheels and ran around whooping. They didn't take the match seriously, as some of the boys did. That afternoon, however, the men stood talking around the horses, subdued and shadow-eyed.

It was the Feast Day of Black Sarah. She was the Gypsies' patron saint. Being their patron saint meant Sarah listened more closely to Rom prayers than to those of anybody else. Praying directly to her increased the chances of a prayer coming true. That day Andrej was praying for a soccer ball of his own. He'd been making necklaces out of painted beads and trying to sell them in towns that they passed, but lately it seemed nobody had need of a necklace, nor patience for the Gypsy boy peddling them. He'd never get a soccer ball without the aid of prayer.

Traditionally, the celebrations in honor of Saint Sarah were noisy affairs. After dipping the saint's black-faced statue in water in homage to Sarah's miraculous sea journey, then offering up heartfelt thanks for the kindnesses she'd done them over the past year—a lame colt made sound, a woman delivered of twins, an ugly grandson finally married—the clan would celebrate. Many of its members hadn't seen one another since the previous Feast Day. There was news to share about births and deaths, gossip to spread about robbery and kisses, hair-raising adventures from the road to act out hilariously. Handiworks were compared, babies were displayed, coins were tossed, dice rolled. Horses were paraded before critical eyes, guitar and violin strings were tuned. Wine barrels were opened, and chickens were slaughtered to roast on spits alongside leaping lambs. The clearing would smell deliciously, and everyone would be happy.

But that day, the day the scarlet kite flew, was different from the gatherings of the past. Everything looked almost as it always did—the freshly painted caravans standing beneath the birches at the clearing's edge, the cart horses hobbled and released to clomp through the weeds; the fires burning, the lambs cooking, the children running, the musicians playing. But the flutes and fiddles rang out less brazenly than usual, and no boisterous husbands were swinging their wives in circles, and no women, elbows linked, were spinning together in a colorful whirl of skirts and sleeves and scarves. Instead, the women were consulting mutedly, reading secrets revealed by tea leaves or the creases of a palm; and the men were more interested in comparing what they'd heard and seen on their travels than in joining their children's soccer game. Everything seemed muffled, as if the glossy day was blanketed in snow.

Andrej knew why.

When the soldiers and the army lorries had first appeared on the road, Andrej's father had told his eldest son not to be so worried. "This is the *gadje's* war, Andrej," he'd said. "It's got nothing to do with the Rom. Let the *gadje* fight each other if they want to: their quarrel won't involve us." Andrej's father had been right—this wasn't a Gypsy war—but he had also been wrong. The war was touching everything, *gadje* or not. Like a roach it was sniffing its way into the smallest corners and lurking there; like a great storm it was sprawling out hugely, darkening the land. Everything it touched it tainted, making ordinary things different from how they'd been—making them difficult, and sometimes dangerous. Everywhere they traveled, Andrej felt the unease.

And here the war was, on this sunny afternoon, in the clearing with the clan on the Feast Day of the saint, leeching the day of its buoyancy. The Rom had no allegiance to either side that was fighting and had nothing to do with the reasons behind the war, nor any wish to be drawn into the conflict: but the roads felt less safe for them now, and sullen glances seemed to turn on them more often, and there was less money to be earned weaving rattan and telling fortunes and shoeing horses, so life had become slightly fragile. There had even been talk of canceling the Feast Day gathering, but such talk had been seen for what it was, a sign that the Rom were bowing to the influence of the *gadje*. And because no one cared for the thought of doing that, the day went ahead as planned; but no one was pretending things were as they had been, and Andrej wondered if he should request of Black Sarah an end to the war, rather than a soccer ball. Everyone said the war would end soon though, so it seemed wasteful to ask.

Andrej, in common with the other children running around the clearing that day, was trying to believe that despite what their eyes and hearts told them, nothing was badly wrong in their world, and that all they had to do was behave themselves, and not pester the adults, and eat what they were given, and everything would become all right.

The last moment of peace and normality that Andrej remembered was of seeing his cousin Nicholae kick the soccer ball hard and high. Nicholae was the best soccer player Andrej had ever seen; his ability had been born with him just as had the port-wine birthmark that lay like a patch over one eye, and he was graceful and artistic, although not above showing off. Ignoring the oncoming charge of his cousins, Nicholae trapped the ball with the point of his toes, then booted it beautifully over the boys' heads. Andrej remembered following the ball's flight toward the clouds and seeing there the scarlet kite, red and clean as a knife wound against the sky, and thinking to himself *Nicholae is showing off* but recalling his mother saying that God gave Nicholae his skill in apology for also giving him the birthmark, and that Andrej wasn't to begrudge his cousin the occasional skite.

The soccer ball, flying like a bullet, jetted into the thick woods that surrounded the clearing, and disappeared. The game came to a jogging halt. Andrej, who was nearest the trees, called, "I'll get it!"

The trees were birch trees, growing close together. Their trunks and branches were slim and white and their leaves were lucidly green, yet a birch forest always seemed denser and less friendly than it should. The air was cool and smelled of stagnancy and rot; the soil was black and slippery, and stuck to the soles of Andrej's feet. He picked his way from trunk to trunk, the hair on his arms lifting with chill. He scanned all about for the soccer ball, but couldn't see it lodged anywhere. He walked deeper into the woods, puzzling. In every direction were peaky tall trees gathered like gaunt spectators to his quest. The earth was too lumpish for the ball to have rolled away, the trees too crowded to have allowed it to bounce far, yet Andrej couldn't see the ball anywhere it should have been.

What he did see was Tomas, sitting cross-legged on a mossy rock, nursing Wilma in his lap. "It's up there." Tomas untucked an arm and pointed to the soccer ball, which had caught in the fork of a tree. "You'll have to climb."

Andrej frowned and asked, "What are you doing here?" even though he knew. Tomas was skulking, as unsocial as ever. Around his family he was as outgoing as a parrot. Unfamiliar faces made him retreat like a snail.

Tomas knew his failing, and did not try to deny it. "Mama told me to take the baby and get out from under her feet."

"Hmm." Andrej imagined their mother's tolerance for her son's clingy ways snapping jaggedly, like a finger. She was worried about the war, Andrej knew. When he was supposed to be sleeping he had heard his parents talking on the steps of the caravan, his mother's voice brittle with entreaty. She wanted to go somewhere far away. There had to be a place too humble to be of interest to the war. His father's frustrating reply was that only *gadje* should be forced to flee a *gadje* war. "Come and play soccer with us," Andrej told his brother. "Nicholae is playing really well."

Tomas shook his head woefully, as Andrej had known he would. "No one lets me kick the ball. I never get given a chance."

"You *make* your chance, Tom, you don't get *given* it —"

"I don't want to." Tomas's mouth set stubbornly.

Andrej sighed, and considered his brother and newborn sister. Wilma was asleep, but her face was white, and a minuscule insect shaped like a sail was walking on her cheek. "At least come out of the woods," he said. "You're being silly."

"No. I like it here."

"But it's cold. Wilma will get sick if you sit here."

Tomas touched the baby's cheek, chased away the sail-shaped bug. Perhaps it dawned on him how much angrier their mother would be if he didn't take proper care of her. "All right." He unfolded a leg that was printed with crimps from the rock. "I'll help you get the ball out of the tree."

And Andrej realized something then—that although he had been wandering around the woods for long minutes, no one had shouted at him to hurry up, and none had ventured to come after him to help with the hunt. He looked over his shoulder toward the clearing, and the strange knowledge came to him that he'd rather be scolded for being an incompetent searcher than hear such silence behind him. "What is it?" Tomas asked, immediately stilled.

Andrej cocked his head. "Can you hear anything?"

Tomas listened. "Only the leaves."

Andrej remembered later the childish thought he'd had at that moment: that the entire clan had packed up the food and instruments and the statue of Black Sarah and hitched the horses and driven off soundlessly, leaving him behind. In the next instant he'd recognized this as merely a child's nightmare, and so hadn't run frantically back to the clearing. He'd walked, and Tomas carrying Wilma had followed him, and the good damp earth of the birch woods had soaked up the noise of their footsteps. "What about the ball?" Tomas asked, and Andrej said, "Shh."

Yet for all his imaginings he had not expected to see what he saw when they reached the fringe of the woods. He didn't know what he expected — something unusual, or maybe nothing so. But he had not expected what was there. He stepped past the last tree into the clearing, then sprang back like a startled cat. "What is it?" said Tomas, and Andrej clamped a hand over his brother's mouth. Tomas's dark eyes rolled up to him, and Andrej saw he understood the need for utter silence, and lowered his hand.

Silent as spiders, hidden in shade, they leaned forward to see beyond the trees.

The clan was grouped in the grassy space where the cooking was done. The adults were lined up in a ragtag row. The children, including the boys who had been playing soccer and the younger ones who'd been flying the kite, were standing near them, herded into a nervous clutch. The scarlet diamond of the kite lay flat in the center of the soccer field, fleetingly catching Andrej's eye.

Standing around the fires, picking at the roast lamb, was a party of soldiers wearing the dusky uniform of the invading army. Andrej counted seven of them. One, older and stronger than the others, was talking, but quite softly, and Andrej couldn't hear. He glanced at Tomas, held a finger to his lips, and motioned him to stay where he was; Tomas, hugging Wilma, shrank like a fox cub to the ground.

Keeping to the forest shadows, Andrej skirted the clearing. As he drew closer to where the clan stood, he could hear the voice of the strong soldier. The man was speaking the invaders' language, which sounded like flying chips of wood. Andrej couldn't understand it, and he knew that his father and mother and Uncle Marin couldn't, and that probably none of the clan could either. The soldiers must have known it too, because the one who was speaking was also waving his arms about to illustrate his words. He tucked his hands into his armpits and flapped his elbows like wings. *"Krähen!"* he said, and his fellow soldiers laughed. "Arrk, arrk! *Krähen!"*

Crows: it was a name the Rom were used to. They heard it on streets and in market squares every day. The clan elders said nothing, shuffling their feet. The flock of children were watching their parents in shifting, edgy confusion. One small child named Klementina broke out with a burble of upset, and made to rush to her mother. A soldier, whirling, shoved her back among the children. *"Nicht weinen!"*

commanded the strong soldier, his voice an ax striking timber. *"Stehen still!"* And Mirabela, who was hardly bigger than Klementina, lifted the smaller girl in her arms and said, "Shh, shh, little one."

Huddled into a shallow of earth, Andrej felt sickening fear. His father said it wasn't the Gypsies' war: yet these soldiers were here, in their boots and caps, shouting at the clan and ordering them about; and each of them carried a rifle, and a pistol in a holster. He scanned the clan for his mother and father and saw them near the end of the line, with Marin, slender and watchful and *young*, younger than Andrej had ever understood, standing beside them. He didn't look afraid, but Andrej knew he must be; even his father, who never faltered, must be slightly afraid. Some of the women began to mumble prayers but the soldier said, *"Ruhig!"* and they stopped.

His mother was so close that Andrej could see smudges where she'd wiped her damp hands on her apron; so close that, had Andrej spoken loudly, she might have heard. The soldiers had lost interest in the roast lamb and were strolling the campsite now, nudging at things with their black-booted toes. One of them found the statue of Black Sarah, and held her up by the throat for the others to see. *"Hässlich wie die Sünde!"* he said, which made his companions laugh. One made gibbering noises, as if Sarah were an ape. The soldier holding the statue gave it a smacking kiss on the lips; then strode to the nearest fire and dumped the statue into the flames.

Old Aunt Emilie, who loved Saint Sarah, bellowed, and cannoned forward. The strong soldier struck her so viciously that she dropped like a stone. Blood splashed as she hit the ground. Someone shouted—Emilie's son, Miki—and jumped out from the line. Quick as a snake, the soldier pulled his pistol and shot Miki in the forehead.

The shot echoed across the clearing. For a moment there was no sound except this ghostly ricochet. The horror of what had happened lurched through the clan, swaying it like a broken bridge. Andrej, in the hollow, pressed his hands to his mouth.

Then the horses hobbled around the caravans whinnied and shied in fear. Some of the children started to scream. The adults reeled as if pushed by a gale, crossing themselves, covering their eyes. The soldiers roared, "*Nein! Nicht sprechen! Stehen still!*"

Miki lay facedown in the weeds. His mother, moaning, grabbed at him, pulling at the collar of his shirt. Somebody went to help the old woman, but stopped when the strong soldier barked, "*Nein!*" The adults looked at the children, pleading at them with their eyes to be quiet and well behaved. The children had clustered tightly together, like sheep. Some were sobbing but the bigger ones hushed them, understanding what was required. Andrej saw Nicholae among them, holding the wrist of his older sister Irena. His naked feet were caked with soil, his black hair was ragged and dusty. In his right ear was a thick hooped earring of which he was very proud. Andrej looked at his mother and saw she was also watching the children. Her green eyes skipped their faces back and forth. She was searching, Andrej realized: searching the children for the ones who were her own.

The soldiers ignored Miki and Emilie. They stared contemplatively around the campsite, rifles slung at the ready. They talked to each other in their cracked-kindling language, pointing to the caravans and the trampled tarot. In the fire, Black Sarah burned, feeding a high orange flame. Andrej's mother continued to scan the children, although by now she must have seen that her own three weren't there. Seen it, but not dared believe.

Then one of the soldiers noticed something. His boots twinkled in the sunlight as he stalked across the clearing. Andrej readied himself to run, but it was not him the soldier had seen. The man snapped his fingers at Nicholae, beckoning him out from amid the children.

No sound was made by anyone, but Andrej felt the clan's spirit plunge the way a wounded deer goes down on its knees. Then, "Don't," said a voice, and Andrej almost jumped up shouting because it was Uncle Marin who had spoken, his precious Marin. "He's only a boy," said Marin.

The soldiers paid no attention. They came together to inspect the claret birthmark encircling Nicholae's eye. Nicholae obligingly tipped his face to the light and Andrej could see that his hands were shaking, flicking loosely against his thighs.

The soldiers poked the mark with their fingers. They spoke thorny words to each other. Their mouths turned down steeply, curious and repulsed. Then they straightened and hedged away, and one of them raised his rifle to Nicholae.

A terrible torn sound came from the Gypsies. "Do not!" shouted Uncle Marin. The soldier with the rifle pivoted, and must have pulled the trigger, because Marin skidded sideways as if he'd stepped on ice. He had fallen to the earth before Andrej could finish thinking, *Don't, he is my friend —*

Andrej's father grabbed Andrej's mother's arm. And somehow, without touching him, Andrej's mother grabbed Andrej. Though he felt as if he had been cut into pieces, Andrej didn't move from the shallow. Though inside him shrilled a thousand agonized screams, he didn't make a sound.

The firing of the rifle did change things, however. A heavy door seemed in some way to close. The soldiers, who had been like spoiled boys, became coolly polished and professional. To the adults who were groaning in despair they crooned, "Shoo, shoo, *Krähen.*" They hustled the children into the arms of their mothers, speaking in businesslike tones. *"Schnell! Kein sprechen! Habt keine Angst."* Mothers drew in sucking breaths as they grappled their offspring to their hips. One soldier beckoned two men out of line, and motioned at the caravans. *"Nehmt eure Schaufeln!"* he said. When he saw that they didn't comprehend, he pantomimed digging the dirt. Even Andrej understood that he wanted the men to fetch the shovels that hung against the sides of the vans.

Many of the younger children were crying, a muddy warble which meant they were frightened and didn't know what was happening. The women petted them, calming them down. The older children and the men were ashen-faced and subdued. Andrej's father was staring at Uncle Marin, whose body lay awkwardly, bent at elbows and knees. His hat had dropped off when he fell. Andrej's mother stood with empty arms, her shining gaze sweeping the woods.

The men collected nine shovels from the caravans, and when the soldier indicated they should pass the tools out to others, Andrej's father was given one.

When everyone in the clearing was finally silent and waiting, the strong soldier looked up from his perusal of the campsite. *"Jetzt!"* he said. *"Habt keine Angst. Folgt diesem Soldaten! Seid still wie eine Maus!"* He made a creeping motion, like a prowling cat. A soldier with a metal star on each shoulder clapped his hands and gestured, and the clan, after a hesitation, turned and shambled through the grass after him. Andrej's aunt Marie helped Emilie up from the ground. The blood that had splashed the old woman's face was redder than the kite. Women walked close to their husbands, holding their children's hands. Four men who weren't bearing shovels were waved out of line and shunted toward the two who lay on the ground. The strong soldier wagged his fingers, indicating that he wanted the bodies carried away.

When they lifted Uncle Marin by his wrists and ankles, his head slung back and Andrej saw his face and thought of all the things he would now never know.

The soldier with the stars on his shoulders led the clan out of the clearing. The Rom trudged after him meekly, as if they wished to be led. Their clothes were bright and rumpled, as they always were. The women had multicolored scarves in their hair, the men wore striped and spotty bandannas round their throats. Some wore leather sandals, but most walked in bare feet. The men carrying the shovels and the men carrying the bodies walked slightly apart from their relatives, closer to the soldiers who sauntered alongside.

Soldiers and Rom headed into the trees on the far side of the clearing. The Rom went in silence, but one of the soldiers was whistling. Andrej sat up on his knees to watch them leave. And saw his mother, at the end of the line, turn back to look into the woods. In a loud fearless voice she called, "Run, children!"

The strong soldier, trailing casually, didn't understand Romany, and thought she was shouting at him. He made a grouching noise and shoved her onward with the heel of his hand.

Andrej stayed in the hollow until his clan and the soldiers had disappeared between the trees and the forest had swallowed them whole, and the horses had lowered their heads to graze and a bird came to peck at a plate. Then he did as his mother told him, and ran.

THE ROAD

The lioness and wolf and bear were lying down in their enclosures, their flanks gently lifting and falling. The monkey, sated to sickness on jam, had retreated to the rear of its cage. The eagle was invisible in its corner; no sound came from the seal's watery cell. The kangaroo dozed on the prop of its tail. The llama and the chamois had folded their legs and looked like rocks in the dark. The boar's cage was overcast with shadow. The moon, held up in Night's great hand, shone lustrously.

Andrej stood to stretch his limbs. He didn't feel tired at all. He and Tomas and Wilma had been walking for weeks, and usually, when they slept, it was like laborers, heavily as soil. They'd wake in a barn or a field and it would be a waking like a rising from the dead. But, perhaps because of the radiance of the moon, tonight he was not tired.

The chamois said, "I don't understand. Your clan wasn't stealing the soldiers' territory. You weren't eating their food. You weren't challenging or threatening them. So why did they attack?"

Andrej answered honestly, "I don't know." In the time they'd spent walking he had pondered countless photographs of missing people tacked to lampposts and brick walls, hoping he might discover in their collective images something that would explain why these people, like his people, should have disappeared. The faces were thin and fat, rich and poor, elderly and youthful, male and female. They smiled or stared out from the photographs, all different, all exactly the same. Studying the images made Andrej more confused, rather than less so. None of them explained why the invaders did what they did. His father said this wasn't a Rom war, but Andrej couldn't believe that it was, instead, the war of these boys, these young women, these old men.

"They called us crows." Tomas, bleary-eyed, raised his head from his knees. "They laughed at our caravans and our statue. They yelled at us. But we weren't doing anything to them. They'd never even met us. They killed my uncle without speaking one word to him. But he was a good man. He used to find coins behind my ear. If they'd talked to him, they would have seen."

"It's no use trying to make sense of what people do." The llama sighed. "Who'd think anyone would want to look at a monkey? Yet people used to come to see him every day."

The wolf spoke up. "I've told you the reason for everything that happens. Somebody decides that they will have their way."

". . . And it *has* to happen, even if their way is wrong?"

"If they are mightier than you, yes."

Tomas returned his chin to his knees to mull this over. His thoughts crinkled his nose. "I don't think that's right, wolf. What if you're smarter than they are? Sometimes you can win by being smarter than everyone else."

"I am smarter than you," replied the wolf, "yet I am locked in this cage, and you're walking around free."

Tomas grinned. "That must mean I'm mightier than you!"

"Well," said the wolf, "we could decide that, if you let me out."

Without lifting her head the lioness asked, "So how have you come from the woods to a zoo? Have you run all the way, Andrej?"

Andrej turned to her, smiling faintly. "No. I only ran back to Tomas. After that, we walked."

His brother had been shuddering with fear when he found him, the baby being shaken in his arms. He had looked saucer-eyed at Andrej and tried to speak, but no words had come out, just a distraught puff of air. Andrej, not knowing what to do, had put his arms around him, muffling his sobs against his chest. The birch trees stood close, waxen and crooked and beautiful. Lively birds hopped from branch to rustling branch. In the fork of a tree, the soccer ball waited.

Then Wilma began to cry. She started off mildly and quickly worked up to a howl. Terrified the soldiers would hear her and return, Andrej had pulled Tomas to his feet. "Get up, Tomy. We have to go." Tomas had been sluggish and reluctant. "What if Mama comes back? She won't know where to find us."

"She told us to run," said Andrej. "She meant *run away*."

They'd picked a path downhill through the woods until they were a good distance from the clearing. Tomas found a nest of mossy boulders and rotten tree limbs, and they waited in its moist cradle for hours. Mosquitoes came for them and needled their flesh. Dirt caked their fingers and toes. A woodpecker tapped out an argument with a neighbor. Tomas and the baby drifted in and out of sleep. Andrej stayed awake listening to far-off comings and goings: the thrum of lorries and motorbikes, the tat-tat of guns fired randomly, the droning of an airplane. The sky stayed blue all afternoon, smoke-streaked to match the children's smudged faces. Thoughts of his mother and father dipped through Andrej's mind like doves coming down to drink. He refused to think about Marin. It was important that he should not cry.

Tomas's eyes dragged open. "I'm hungry."

Andrej had already decided what to do. "Stay here. I'm going back to the clearing. There might be food there. I'll be back soon, I promise."

His brother nodded druggedly, too exhausted to protest. Trusting too, Andrej realized: Tomas had made the decision to trust his brother with his life. The burden weighed Andrej down immedi-ately. "Take care of Wilma," he said, so it was fair.

It was a long steep climb back through the forest. Sometimes he scrambled on hands and knees. He remembered their cart horse, Flower, snorting as she'd pulled the caravan along the road that led to the clearing. Andrej and his father had climbed down and walked so she would have less of a load to pull. It had happened only that morning, but seemed something recalled from when Andrej was small.

Flower wasn't in the clearing; none of the horses were. The ropes that had hobbled them were lying severed in the grass. The caravans had been half-heartedly torched and stood listing on charred wheels or collapsed onto their axles, their bowed ribs showing through ragged canvas. The Rom's goods were scattered about — frying pans, cups and plates, paintbrushes, strings of beads, hair combs, farrier tools, dented buckets, wooden toys — some broken and soiled, some safe and whole. The roast lambs had vanished from the spits, but chunks of white chicken remained. The grass underfoot was knotted and trampled. There was a smell of smoke and scorched wool.

Andrej stood amid the wreckage, the last of the day's sunshine beaming on his head and the birds chirping to one another, feeling as if his life had slipped off him like a coat and that his heart was exposed to the air.

The statue of Black Sarah lay in a pyre of coals; Andrej pawed her onto the grass and rolled her around to cool her. The lower half of her body was burned and broke away in chunks, which he swept together into a pyramid and tried to clean with the palms of his hands. Part of him watched himself in bemusement, aware he was doing something useless, knowing he'd deliberately lost track of what he should be doing. "Help me, Sarah," he whispered, and his voice sounded odd, watery. Something glimmered in the corner of his eye, and the statue slipped from his mind. The glimmering was Marin's blood puddled on the earth. Andrej walked close enough for his toes to touch it. The blood was not red, but a shade of ruby-black. It was not wet, but leathery, nearly dry. Andrej saw a dim reflection of himself shift across it.

"He is dead." He told the birds that Marin was dead. They flitted, full of life, between the branches. He asked, "Where has everyone gone?"

The forest showed no sign that the clan had ever passed through it. Andrej wandered among the trees, his bare arms going to gooseflesh as he moved away from the reach of the sun and into the verdant shadows. The undergrowth compressed beneath his feet with ancient sighs. His finger-tips skimmed saplings, twiggy branches, grizzled catkins, flimsy leaves.

He walked so deeply into the woods that the clearing was smothered from view and the sky crisscrossed by pearly branches before he realized that he knew what he was looking for, and that, if he kept walking, he would find it.

The soldiers had driven their prisoners into wilderness. They hadn't taken them down a road or a trail because it didn't matter where they were going, they weren't going somewhere or anywhere. They were going to a place that was nowhere.

Andrej stopped, and his hands floated down to rest on the frail peak of a birch yearling. In every direction gaped silence. The trees clustered round him like sad narrow ghosts. He rocked on his toes, said soft words to himself. He was empty and helpless and afraid, a statue of a boy thrown into the sea or left behind to be swallowed by the desert.

It was the thought of Tomas and Wilma that got him moving again. They would be hungry and fretful. But the strange thing was that Andrej suddenly craved to return to them. He needed to see his brother and sister with a desperation that sang. He turned on his heels and ran.

In the clearing he moved quickly, ducking from caravan to caravan salvaging anything he could find that seemed useful. He found tins of beef that the soldiers had overlooked, and a net bag of apples and beans. He found a pan of water in which stood a jug of still-fresh cream. He found coats and boots that would fit boys, and the necessities of babies.

In secret compartments in each caravan, he found money. He found a keen folding knife, and wares he might trade, bangles and earrings and hat pins. He packed two sacks until he had as much as he could carry. He gave no thought to those who had owned what he found. He hid the money carefully in the packs. He dressed himself in warm clean clothes and shoes. Lastly he gathered the chicken from the spits and the bread from the dirt, and started down the hill.

Passing the kite, which lay in the grass, Andrej knew with an abrupt and unquestionable certainty that it was the kite which had brought the soldiers to the clearing. From a long way off it would have been visible, weaving brilliant as a beacon above the trees. In the nights to come, he would dream of kites lifting him into the sky.

Tomas thought they should wait and wait, because the alternatives seemed difficult and draining and something they might regret; but by the next morning Andrej had chivvied him into walking. They needed water, and milk for Wilma, and they wouldn't get it in these woods which had already proved how unsafe they could be. "Besides," said Andrej cajolingly, "if we walk we might find someone. We might find Papa." He didn't ask if Tomas believed this could happen, and Tomas never mentioned the possibility again.

They were accustomed to traveling, and perhaps this made easier the many days and weeks that followed. All their lives had been lived on the road, and it was natural and expected that each morning should bring something new. The road itself was as it had always been: either wide and winding and cut from the earth, or long and cramped and lined with red bricks. On either side of it spread fields sprouting green crops, the farms interrupted occasionally by small farmhouses and big barns and villages that were hardly more than a handful of timber homes. In some places it was easy to believe that the war was something they'd imagined: women and children strolled about doing chores, men smoked pipes out of open windows, puppies romped from doorways to greet them, and everything seemed usual, unchanged. In other places, however, where enemy had clashed with enemy, the war had left great claw marks on the land, and these places were unspeakably awful. Fields stretched smoldering and smoky to the horizon, coils of barbed wire tangling across them, every tree cut down. Dead cows lay in oily puddles, bloated taut and huge; horses sagged killed in their traces, their carts shattered behind them. Bridges were drowned, streets were torn up, houses were on fire and spilling gizzards of bedheads, kitchen tables, bathtubs, typewriters. The air was hazy, smelling of metal and grease and of something grayer and meaner too. One morning, in a village larger than many, they saw people lying higgledy-piggledy, their arms and legs bent in ways that reminded Tomas of puppets and Andrej, chokingly, of Uncle Marin. Their mortal wounds made the children look away to the piles of sandbags, the raided shop fronts, the fountain with its broken stone bowl. In another town, where mattresses had been chunked against windows and walls, they found an abandoned antitank gun and played on it for most of the afternoon. The gun was, the brothers agreed, the best thing they'd ever seen.

They rarely stopped anywhere for longer than a few hours or a night. They rested when footsore or when Wilma was riled. Andrej didn't know where they were going—he did not think it mattered. When they'd lived in the caravan they had gone where the road took them, and this was what they did now, choosing the path that seemed to promise the best prospects for food or solitude or sunshine. Andrej tried not to think about what was behind them and what waited ahead, sensing the crippling error in dwelling too closely on their situation. It was better just to march on as if this was exactly what two boys and a baby were supposed to be doing. Andrej carried the heavier pack while Tomas bore the smaller one, into which they had tucked Wilma. At first she had argued forcibly against the sack; gradually she came to like it. They spent money when they had to, mostly on fresh milk for the baby, but usually they scrounged for what they could find in deserted houses and unguarded fields. Sometimes they traded sparkly trinkets to the people who still had use for such gewgaws; they met beggars, but without the protection of an adult it felt unwise for them to likewise beg. They filled their flask from pumps in towns, and bathed in marshy lakes while geese flew overhead honking opinions forthrightly. They crossed the paths of other Rom occasionally, but these were unrelated strangers and took only the briefest notice of the children. Andrej saw no reason to ask for their help: so far, he thought they were faring well enough on their own. They never spoke to the *gadje* unless they had to, and the *gadje* rarely spoke back except to hustle them along. There were many refugees traveling the roads, some driving carts or pushing them, others on coughing tractors or in open cars, some riding squeaky bikes or trudging horses, others stumbling along on their feet. Some were injured, some seemed numbed, all were troubled and aggrieved. In its destructive push across the country, the war had taken from these luckless souls the mainstays of their lives, their homes and work and neighborhoods, their intentions for a future. Amid this shifting, sunken-eyed crowd, three scrappy Gypsy children were of no interest at all.

But one day, an old woman tried to take Wilma. She plucked the infant from Andrej's arms saying, "You can't take care of her." Andrej froze with astonishment: it was Tomas who shrieked like a wildcat and leapt like one too, fastening himself to the crone's shoulder. "*Our* baby!" he'd wailed, fists flying like cat paws. Andrej had unfrozen to snatch his startled sister from her abductor, who slapped at Tomas until he dropped off like a tick. "Keep her then!" the ghastly stranger had shouted. "The soldiers will take care of her! They're looking for people like you. Dirty little leeches. Filthy nasty robbers. Vermin, you are! Heathen vermin! The sooner they get rid of the likes of you, the better off we'll be."

The confrontation spooked Andrej so badly that he found shelter in a church loft and stayed there for two days. The children were used to being called names—despising the Rom was a timeless amusement of the *gadje*. Andrej had once asked his father why this was so, and his father explained, "People jeer at those who are different from themselves—those who look different, or think differently, or live in different ways. They do it because difference is a frightening thing—sometimes, an enviable thing." Was this what the woman had felt—fear of them, and envy? Andrej couldn't believe it. It had been something much worse than that. Something like a monster finally escaped from chains.

Tomas, recovering from his initial shock, chose to pretend the old woman was Baba Jaga, the legendary flying witch who stole children, and occasionally ate them. "Get back to your horrible house, Baba Jaga!" he cried, chopping at the dusty sunlight that shafted through the church windows. The attack he'd launched upon the crone was the first real stance he had taken against the will of the world. Victory made him arrogant for days, as well as somewhat awed.

To Andrej, however, the encounter brought an understanding that they were in a special kind of danger, a peril far more fearsome than any crackle-faced hag from a fairy tale. He thought over and over on what the old woman had said. *The sooner they get rid of the likes of you.* This was what the soldiers in the clearing had been doing: getting rid of the likes of the clan. For some unfathomable reason, the invading army felt such . . . *hatred* . . . of the Rom that they would kill a man like Marin as readily as they'd swat a bug. And some of the *gadje* who'd always lived in this land, shoulder to shoulder with the Rom—people like the Baba Jaga woman and who knew how many more—were eager to have it done.

Andrej, lying awake in the airless loft while fire-flies tapped on the window's clouded glass, came to see that loneliness and confusion were midges in comparison with the threat that was really stalking them. The monster that had escaped its chains had countless arms and legs and eyes and mouths, innu-merable shapes and disguises; and it was merciless even to mothers and children, even to the best of men. *They're looking for people like you.*

He saw they must never trust anybody. It would be too easy to become snared. They must avoid other Rom, whose company would attract attention. They must stay alert and invisible and on the move. Something was seeking them.

Andrej had reached across and shaken Tomas, who'd sat up woozily from his pillow of boots. "Come," Andrej told him. "We're leaving." Already he burned to be on their way.

From that night onward the children traveled when darkness could conceal them and fewer people were about, stopping for brief rests or to attend Wilma, then walking on into the dawn. During the day they hid and slept, emerging only if they needed to buy some essential. Baba Jaga had called them *leeches, robbers, vermin,* and although Mama and Papa and Marin and Nicholae and Emilie and Mirabela and none of the others were any of those things, Andrej was happy for his siblings and himself to become rats—sleeping by day, moving by night, raiding and rummaging, staying out of sight. Rattiness would be their protecting charm. Marin had always said, "It's a lucky soul that gets put into a rat."

Hearing his uncle's voice in his head made Andrej cover his ears. His heart mourned for Marin through every moment, even in his dreams. He pined for the comfort of his mother, the steadfast presence of his father. But Tomas was always there, hungry and jovial and querulous, and Wilma with her round head and button eyes caused practical problems which distracted him countless times a day. When Andrej slept, he slept catatonically. When awake, he was thinking constantly, vigilant to every threat, ceaselessly devising ways to outwit and outrun. And so, although the pain of what he'd lost was ever-present and severe, Andrej had no time for stopping to look long at it, or for looking back.

THE TEST

"*Wah-wah-wah,*" said the chamois. "No life is without its troubles, kid, not even the life of a rat. Look on the bright side: you aren't in a cage. You're free, so stop complaining."

Andrej, startled from his memories, said, "No, I'm not in a cage, but—I don't *feel* free. If you're free, you should be safe. And I don't feel safe. I always feel . . . hunted."

"Boo-hoo," said the chamois rancorously. "Talk to me about being hunted when you find your foot in a snare, little buck."

The llama's tufted ears turned: "How peculiar! You can go anywhere your feet take you, and yet you're not free. There are no bars around you, yet you're in a funny kind of cage. *That* isn't fair."

"Cages come and get you," murmured the kangaroo.

Andrej said nothing; Wilma was in his arms, and he rocked her. The baby was placidly tasting her fingers, peering out from deep in the shawl. Though he'd struggled valiantly to stay awake, Tomas's eyelids had begun to droop and eventually he had fallen asleep on the bench, feet tucked securely out of reach of any boar. He lay with his hands folded under his cheek, small inside his clothes. Moonlight was tinting the maple leaves white, and draped the grass like a frayed sheet of linen. The light was luminous, but not as crisp as it had been. The world was still veiled by darkness, but the brief summer night had begun its tender bloom into day. Soon peace would end.

The lioness spoke. "Your mother would be proud of you, Andrej. You have taken care of your brother and sister. You have done what she wanted you to do."

Andrej winced. He hated to remember the boy crouched in the woods watching his mother being led away. "I should have run *to* her, instead of running away. I might have been able to help her."

"No. That isn't what she wanted."

Wilma mumbled, and Andrej looked at her. He wondered if his tiny sister would grow up to look like her mother—tall, with painted nails and bony feet, and dark hair that reached down her spine. Andrej could remember these things about his mother, but he was forgetting, too. It was hard to hear her voice, or to picture her green eyes and white smile. He could no longer see whole pieces of her—her hands and elbows, her hay-fevery nose. His mother had been taken from the clearing, and from his memory. When Wilma was grown she might indeed look like her mother, but Andrej would have forgotten how to know for sure. Quietly, so as not to disturb Tomas, he said, "I don't think they will come back. I don't think I'll see them again."

"No," the lioness agreed.

"Do you think the owner of the zoo will come back?"

"No."

"What about Alice?"

Alice! The word whisked through the air more urgently than before. *Alice, Alice:* the animals moved fitfully, shifting their weight, scuffing their feet on the stone. They were calling to her, their cries resounding into emptiness. The lioness said nothing.

Andrej sighed. Tipping his chin, he looked up at the sky. The stars were glinting studs against the sapphire clouds. Uncle Marin had known the names of the constellations. He had known, too, which shining dots weren't stars, but red and yellow and purple planets. Sometimes he'd said, *I wonder what is happening on the purple planet today?*

Andrej looked at the lioness, who hadn't moved. The moonlight made aqua pools of her eyes, smooth golden velvet of her coat. "Do you think the lion and your cubs will come back?"

"No."

"How do you know?"

"I feel it," she said, "as you do."

Andrej nodded. There was sorrow in him so boundless and powerful that he hardly dared approach it. If it got loose, it would gallop like a bolting horse through a fairground, overturning everything it touched. Very cautiously he asked, "Did you say good-bye?"

"No."

"I didn't either . . . I can't remember the last things I said to them. It must have been silly things like, *Come and play soccer, Papa,* and *I'm not hungry yet, Mama.*"

The lioness cupped her ears, considering him. After a time she said, "Wherever they are, they know you would have helped them if you'd been able. They know you would have said good-bye."

Andrej bit his lip, and nodded again. "All right."

The lioness continued to watch him. In the cage beside her, the monkey uttered a low groan. The seal broke the surface, sniffed up air and submerged; the water closed over it with a slurp. Beyond the zoo's gate, in what remained of the town, a broken-backed rafter swooned from roof to ground with a muffled crump of noise. Then there was silence. The animals' breathing made no sound. The moonlight touching Andrej's hands looked like powdered crystal. The lioness rose liquidly to her paws. "Andrej," she said, "bring the baby to me."

Andrej lifted his head and gazed at her, but did not get to his feet.

"Just for a moment," said the lioness: in a single stride she had reached the bars and was hovering behind them, her yellow face scarred and eternal. "Not for longer than a moment."

Andrej looked down to his sister, and it crossed his mind how much easier the past weeks would have been if the baby had gone into the woods with her mother with whom she belonged, with whom she wanted to be. So many long years must pass before she could think for herself and look after herself, and he already had Tomas to tend to. Andrej's mind thought these things, and was wearied just by thinking them, but his legs were lead and didn't move. "No," he said stolidly. "I mustn't."

The lioness dodged with agitation, yearning toward the bundled shawl. "It won't hurt. I promise. All you need do is bring her near."

Andrej wavered, worried he might cry. The animals were watching, and he could feel the lioness's longing, and his blood was surging and he wanted to help her but, "I can't," he moaned.

"Why not?" Her tail slashed in frustration; she reared up briefly on two legs. "What harm will it do? Andrej, bring her!"

"No." He shook his head in defiance, his eyes welling with tears. "I won't. I can't." And suddenly he was shouting like a child gone mad: "I won't! I'm frightened of you! You can't have her! She belongs to me!"

"*Idiot boy.*" The words crossed the lawn like flying ice picks, yanking Tomas from his sleep as they speared past, snarled out in a voice so terrifying that it tore the breath from Andrej and he spun to face it believing that the soldier from the clearing had finally come for him. Staring wild-eyed he saw nothing except the stark circle of bars and the maple and frosted grass, but the animals were on their feet and gazing into the stygian core of the zoo: into the wild boar's cage. "Idiot boy," said the voice from that blackness, and Andrej, heart hammering, imagined the creature hidden there, its spindly legs and outlandish head, its arched tusks and bristling hide. "What are you worrying about? You think your precious piglet is too good for a lioness? What harm can she, behind bars, do to you, lounging free? What can she do that would be worse than what you've done to her?"

"Andrej . . ." whimpered Tomas, but Andrej, shielding Wilma, held up a silencing hand. He stared into the darkness that consumed the boar's cage, each muscle ready to move. If the beast was free—if the lock had rusted or the creature had shredded the bars and now was loose and coming for him—Andrej would stand his ground. He was not afraid; his heart, still pounding, beat with a blind sense of outrage. He glanced at the cages surrounding the boar's, saw the wolf, the chamois, the llama. Even if they could help him, Andrej knew they would not. They understood that life is a battle fought alone. And Andrej, in that moment, was ready to fight—he was eager for it. All the injustice he'd suffered was clenching in his fist and prickling in his eyes. He would endure nothing more in dumb helplessness. If the boar came for him, he would hurt it as much as he could. He would kill it if he was able.

But from the boar's cage came nothing, no scuffle of feet nor snort of hot breath, nothing but the voice which was like satin under a millstone, silky and bruised and ruined.

"She was only a cub, that lioness, when a hunter shot her mother so he could tell a tale of changing something fierce and glorious into something humbled and hideous. He stove in the heads of her littermates because he deemed a swift death beneath his boot the kindest thing for them. He spared her, the smallest cub, and sent her across the ocean as a gift to his fiancée. It was important that his beloved be seen to have the best of everything — and what could be better than a lion cub? What he failed to remember, that foolish hunter, is that even a runt lion is still a lion."

Andrej stared into the shadows, scarcely breathing. Tomas, on the bench, had burrowed into his jacket. The wolf's silver hackles were raised.

"The bride-to-be was delighted with her new pet. None of her friends owned such a prize, so they were all satisfyingly jealous. The cub was dressed in ribbons and bows, and when dining on the choicest cuts she wore a little bib. At night she slept on the bride-to-be's bed, and when the dew was off the grass in the morning she was walked around the garden at the end of a velvet cord. She chased peacocks over manicured lawns, and marzipan mice across great halls. She was driven through cities in open-roofed cars so people on the streets could marvel at her. When the jealous friends or regal guests came to visit, she was brought out to entertain them. If she played like a kitten and made everyone smile, she was given a slice of butter. If she hid or hissed or struggled or bit, she was given a little smack. Her world was a rich one, finely dressed and perfumed. She could not have asked for more affection or better care. But a lion in a spoiled lady's boudoir is still a lion, isn't she?"

It was not a question, and Andrej said nothing. The llama shuddered, blinking wide eyes.

"Time passed. The cub was growing. She had never done anything a lion does — never feasted on zebra, never lapped from a lake, never roared to her sisters across a sunstruck plain—but the marrow of her bones knew what she was, and what she'd been born to do. Her claws knew, her teeth knew. Her pride knew.

"Soon came the day when the bride-to-be would become the bride. The hunter had returned from his bloody jaunts, the church was frothy with flowers, the priest and the guests were gathering. Naturally, the bride wanted her wedding to be the talk of the season. Months earlier she had visited the jeweler and ordered a diamond-encrusted collar and leash. Now, shut in a room to one side of the church while the guests shuffled into their pews, the girl in her ivory dress and veil asked that the cub be brought to her. The idea was that the bride should be accompanied down the aisle not just by her father but by the tamed beast as well, this symbol of beauty and freedom subdued, of splendor captured and contained.

"The animal that was brought to her was hardly a cub any longer, however. The cat was a yearling, bigger than any dog, with big clumsy paddles of paw concealing claws that could carve marble. What the cub thought of the white, towering, lace-veiled spectacle that was her mistress we don't need to wonder, given what happened next. The wedding day did become the talk of the season, but not for the right reasons.

"In a life filled with bewildering, unnatural sights, this anemic specter was the one which changed a lion cub into a lioness. As the ghostly bride reached down to fasten the diamond collar, the petrified beast lashed out a paw, and opened the bride's face from ear to ear."

One of the animals breathed harshly, trampling the stone. An old maple leaf dislodged and made a papery sound as it tumbled from branch to branch. Wilma burbled, and the boar paused to listen. Then it went on.

"Can you picture the scene, boy? The rents torn through the veil. The porcelain cheeks slashed by arching wounds, elegant as a poet's flourish.

Ruby blood flowing in sheets from these wounds, swamping the heirloom pearls. Rivers of crimson pouring down the white bodice, flooding the layers of dress. The diamond collar dropping with a dainty *clink* to the floor. The scream that flew out the door like a kestrel, soaring up into the rafters. The confused rush and flutter of the guests. The face of the hunter when he saw his beloved, her loveliness erased. Can you picture it in your mind, boy? Because the hunter always would. He'd see the spitting cub and the flailing bride, both of them pressed in horror to the floor, two lives in which he'd meddled and now must stir himself to muddle further, because he could never marry a disfigured woman, and the beast must face the consequences of being born a vicious lion. Off he marched, wax-faced with affront, to fetch the one thing in the world that would never disappoint him: his gun.

"Oddly enough, it was the bride who saved her. Perhaps the girl had more respect for the creature than she'd shown in front of her friends. Perhaps she was genuinely fond of the animal, and understood the blow had been dealt not in malice, but fear. Perhaps she knew that she too, now forever marred, faced a future in which her happiness relied on the mercy of others. Who knows? Whatever her reason, she stayed the hunter's hand. Maybe he would have ignored her, given that he loved shooting things more than he loved her. But the wedding guests and the priest were there, and his agonized ex-fiancée was arguing for the cat's life, and under the circumstances it would not have looked gentlemanly to tell her to shut her mouth.

"And so the cub who was now a lioness was cast out from that lush life, and sent here, to this end-of-the-road place, and put in a cage which was hung with a sign that said WARNING: LION BITES. Because there *was* a lion in the cage, the first she'd ever seen; but her leonine teeth and bones recognized him, as his teeth and bones recognized her. In each other, they saw the dusty plains, the stumbling zebra, the swampy drinking pool. In the lion's noble shadow she left behind the petted plaything she had been and became instead a true lioness, who heard in her ears the rattle of sandstorms, whose whiskers were blown by the churning monsoon. A true lioness who lived in a cage, doomed to pace the bars without cease, searching for something she knew, yet couldn't see. But in time there came three young of her own, and the company of these and of the lion brought her some serenity. In the wriggling cubs was the proof that, despite the iron bars and the staring faces and the jeweled leashes and the marzipan mice, she was and always had been lion to her core. When she closed her eyes, she saw sweeping visions of magnificence. She saw all things that lions have seen since the first lion left its paw prints on the land. Her life would never be as she would wish it, but the great tribe of lion had not forgotten her.

"But then you started your war, boy, and nothing is as important as what humans want, is it? Nothing is as important as what humans do. You took the lion and the cubs from her as easily as you had taken her littermates and the zebra and the plains. She stood where she is standing now and watched them pushed onto a truck and driven away; she heard them calling until the road unrolled far enough to take even their voices from her. And now she's a lioness locked in a zoo, and at night she looks at the stars and wonders if the tribe has, in fact, forsaken her, though all her life she's been true. And now *you*, you wretched boy, refuse her the sight of your squealing piglet, as if a piglet is too treasuresome to go anywhere near the likes of lion — all the while waging your war with such enthusiasm for death, such carelessness for life, that it's clear nothing on earth is precious in your eyes. What makes that baby an exception? Amid such carnage, what matters the fate of one more? You disgust me, boy." The boar gave a slight, low snicker. "You claim to be different from the *gadje*, but you aren't. Humans are all exactly the same. Each of you lives in a fever of selfishness and destruction. You persecute the creatures that you fear, yet the species you should fear most is your own. I hope this war buries every one of you. Oblivion is clearly what you want, and I hope your wish is fulfilled."

The animals stood like exquisite sculptures in their cages, moonlight pouring from their muzzles, their shadows cast onto the ground as if something of their wild natures was seeping over the stone. Tomas sat in rigid silence, his sights riveted to Andrej, who stood staring across the grass into the blackness of the boar's cage. A piercing like a poison thorn was dragging down Andrej's spine. He didn't know if the boar was free, if he must fight or would be spared, and he stood watching for the smallest movement, listening for the faintest sound . . . But then he saw that such guardedness was unnecessary. Even if the boar was loose, it wasn't going to attack him. The boar *wanted* him to stand there, pinned beneath moonlight and the unflinching gaze of the animals, drenched by accusations, dredging for more courage than he owned. It had cornered him into making a choice he didn't want to make, into proving something he feared to prove. It wouldn't do anything that would allow him to shirk his decision, or earn him their audience's pity.

But I'm only a boy, Andrej wanted to protest. *What have I done? What can I do?*

Wilma gurgled, and he glanced at her. She had extricated a hand from the shawl and was wagging it at him, and Andrej heard himself think distantly that the lioness was right: his mother *would* be proud of how he'd cared for his brother and sister. Looking at them, she would see how he'd tried.

He lifted his head, and his gaze circled the iron-bar wall of the zoo. The animals were watching him, tense and unmoving. Andrej stared back at them, feeling suddenly mulish, standing his ground. He would not be bullied by a pig into offering his sister to a hungry cat.

But there are many kinds of hungers. The eagle, the bear, the monkey, and the seal; the wolf, the chamois, the llama, and the kangaroo; the lioness and Andrej, and Tomas and Wilma, and doubtlessly even the boar: all these had an echoing place inside them from which something vital was now missing. Andrej remembered the boy he'd been such a short time ago — a boy who had trusted that the world was strict but fair. Since then he had seen this faith upended and made laughable. In this new world, a kite could betray the children who played in its skimming shadow. A soldier was not an honorable warrior, but one who chose his victims from among the innocents. A woman would steal a baby, a man would obliterate a town. This wasn't a world that made sense to Andrej: it was a hard wintry shell of a world, bare of compassion.

Yet for all that, he still trusted. It amazed him to discover it: that underneath his grief and dis-enchantment, his belief in a good world was still there. And the more difficult it became to find the goodness, the more certain he was in his faith that it was there.

He turned away from the boar's cage, sure now that even with his back to it, the creature would not come for him. The lioness was standing in the corner of her cage, the moonlight laying stripes across her body. She watched him step closer, one step, another. A lioness is something distinctly *other* than a boy, but, close now, Andrej saw what it was they shared: a determination to endure.

He shifted Wilma until she was sitting in his arms, the shawl peeled back from her face, her tiny hand tucked away. Then he lifted her up to the bars, so near that her forehead knocked the iron. The lioness was there instantly, all lashing tail and shivery muscle and cool, secretive eye. She pushed her face against the bars, her whiskers and jaw and heavy brow, her black lips and scarred snout and snowy chin. This near to her, Andrej smelled an ocher heat rising from her body, as if she'd spent a long day languishing beneath a searing sun.

Her nose was tawny and angular, as wide as a man's palm. It nudged Wilma's face and the bristling muzzle must have tickled, because the baby grimaced and snuffled. The lioness breathed in the infant's scent and breathed it out again loudly, ruffling the baby's sparse hair. Once more she breathed, and Andrej felt the warm air gale past him—air that had been inside a lion, had moved through her heart and mind.

Her muzzle wrinkled, and Andrej saw a glimpse of teeth and pale tongue. "They smell the same," the lioness murmured. "My cubs smelled as she does. Like pollen." She breathed deeply again, and Andrej saw the missing cubs returning to her on the wings of the baby's perfume. "All young ones must come from the same place," she said, then sat down on her haunches, seemingly satisfied.

THE KEYS

Dawn was coming. Night, who had been watching so closely, heard the feather-footed approach of Day in the east and drew his black steed nearer, ready to ride without effort away. The moon, which at midnight had shimmered so majestically, now seemed made of the dullest cloth. The sky that had been cobalt-blue was fading to the floury gray that would become clean morning. Dew gathered on the bars of the cages, and the kangaroo licked it up. The eagle on its perch shook its burden of wings. Smoky light slunk into the boar's enclosure and found nothing to settle upon but a heaped pile of straw and the biscuits that Andrej had put into the cage. Tomas, sitting on the bench swinging his legs to keep warm, kept a wary eye on this pile of straw. For as long as he watched, not a strand of it shifted. The boar could be hiding under there, or it might have used the last of the dark to reach the pebbled path unseen and escape along the road from there. . . . Tomas wasn't sure which he preferred.

Andrej's bag had been repacked with the siblings' valuables and vital goods. Wilma had been fed what was left of her milk, had had her stale swaddling changed, and been nursed by Tomas until she'd fallen asleep. She lay now in the nest of

Tomas's pack, ready to be carried anywhere. She would sleep until the middle of morning, and when she woke she would be dirty and thirsty, needing everything to be done again.

Andrej sat down on the bench beside Tomas, who didn't stop swinging his legs. "Tom, we have to go."

Tomas looked at him. He knew that, after the encounter with Baba Jaga, his brother had vowed never to be caught in open daylight again. Nevertheless he asked, "Can't we stay?"

"No. We need to find food."

It was a good reason, one Tomas couldn't deny. His stomach was grumbling. But, "We can find food in the village, and come back here," he suggested.

Andrej shook his head. "There's nothing to eat in the village. You know that. The mice and birds will have taken everything that wasn't bombed to pieces. Even if we did find something, it wouldn't be enough. It wouldn't be milk for Wilma."

Tomas's eyes slid accusingly to where his sister slept in the pack. His gaze stalked around the zoo then, and Andrej saw all that tussled within him. "I don't want to, Andrej."

"That's what you said before." Andrej smiled. "First you said you didn't want to come here, and now you say you don't want to leave."

Tomas pouted, ignoring this. The animals were moving lethargically behind the bars, stretching their muscles, licking their paws, sniffing the coming day. The wolf yawned redly. The llama shook its ears. In the light, the creatures were poorer than the night had made them seem. Their bones showed, their coats were scurfy, their cages looked small and unclean. Tomas's face creased in vexation. "We *can't* leave them." He whispered it harshly. "It's not right, Andrej!"

"I know."

"There's no one to take care of them!"

"No, I know."

"They need help!"

"I know, Tom."

"So what will we do?"

Andrej said, "We'll set them free."

Tomas gasped, and ogled his brother, who was brave and kind and capable of miracles and who would *never* have abandoned the animals to their fate, Tomas was ashamed he'd thought otherwise: scrambling to his knees he gabbled, "Yes! How? How can we?"

Andrej shrugged. "These are cages, so there must be keys. We'll find the keys and let them out, and they're smart enough to find their way home."

Tomas looked wildly around the zoo, wringing his fingers with excitement. He pictured the kangaroo bouncing round the maple, the monkey racing gymnastically through the leaves. "They won't bite us, will they?" he asked, suddenly unsure; Andrej shook his head and Tomas, feeling foolish, said, "No, I didn't think so. We'll open the cages and they'll just run away. They probably won't even look back. The eagle can fly. What about the seal?"

Andrej hesitated, his dark eyes dipping, and Tomas saw he'd forgotten about the seal. They couldn't leave it alone in the zoo swimming back and forth, back and forth until, like a shadow at dusk, there was nothing left of it; yet nor could they haul it from the pool to hobble awkwardly through the broken timber of villages and burnt stubble of the countryside. Tomas watched his brother thinking, his gaze following his thoughts as they moved around the problem. "Uncle Marin would know what to do," he prompted.

"A cart!" Andrej snapped his fingers. "We'll find a cart, and put the seal in it, and push the cart to a river, and the seal can swim down the river to the sea!"

"Clever!" Tomas rejoiced.

Andrej stepped from the bench. "Let's tell the wolf."

The dying night had turned the wolf's russet coat the sleety gray of storms. The animal sat up watchfully as they approached. Stopping at the bars, Andrej wrapped his hands around the iron. "Wolf, Tomas and Wilma and I can't stay. Soldiers are looking for us. But we're not going to leave you trapped here. We're going to open the cages and let you out. I know you won't attack us. You and the bear and the chamois can find your way home to the mountains. The boar can go too, if it likes. The eagle can fly away. Maybe the lioness and the llama and the kangaroo and the monkey can go with you to the mountains. I know it's not their home, but it's better than being here, alone, in the zoo. We'll put the seal into a cart and take it to a river. There's one not far from here. It can swim down the river to the ocean. Then you'll all be free."

In the wolf's honey-colored eyes the mountains appeared, stark and windswept. The zoo animals looked at each other through the bars, the bear raising its rumpled head. "Did he say they're opening the cages?"

"He said they'll open the cages!"

"I heard him, he said it —"

"That's what he said, they're opening the cages —"

"They're opening the cages, they're letting us out!" The chamois sang it gleefully, prancing in a circle. The monkey screeched and pounced skyward, haring across the bars. The lioness trotted the perimeter of her cage, puffing out brisk roars.

Tomas was jumping up and down, the eagle was pacing its perch. The chamois stopped prancing, and started demanding. "You must let me out first! I'll need a head start on that cat!"

The bear shuffled until it was sitting up. "Are you sure it will be safe?"

Andrej turned to the big animal. "No, it won't be safe. It will be dangerous. The mountains are far away, and the war is everywhere between here and there. You'll need to travel at night, and be careful. Stay away from people, and don't talk to them. There will be lots of danger—but it's dangerous to stay here, too. There's soldiers here. There's rumble-things. You're helpless in these cages."

"I will be scared," the kangaroo decided.

"Don't be scared!" Tomas cried; his heart bled for the little beast. "You won't be scared, you'll be free!"

"Freedom always *sounds* nice." The llama spoke up primly. "But is it clever? If we leave the zoo, who'll take care of us? Who'll bring food and water? Who will change the straw? Where will I sleep? What will I do when it rains? What if I get lonely — who will I talk to? What if something bad happens — what if I fall down a hill?"

"You'll take care of yourself!" Tomas flung up his arms with the simplicity of it. "You'll learn how to do it. Everybody learns to look after themselves. When I was young, I couldn't tie my laces: but then I learned, and now I can!"

"These kids have looked after themselves for two turns of the moon," said the chamois with disdain. "If they can survive on what meager brains *they* have, one imagines *you* can too."

"We could look after each other," offered the kangaroo, but the llama was not reassured. "I'd rather stay here. It sounds too scary."

"It *is* scary, sometimes," Tomas admitted. "But the scary bits are what make you brave."

"You'll just have to believe us," said Andrej. "You're not supposed to have iron bars around you — no one is supposed to have that. You're *supposed* to fall down hills and get lonely, and find your own food and get wet when it rains. That's what happens when you're alive."

"When you're filling your space," said the bear.

"It *can* be frightening, but underneath it's fine. Like the sun is fine on a nice day, you know?"

The llama looked determinedly doubtful; then, the next instant, reflective. It said, "Sometimes I have a dream that I'm eating blue flowers. They are very tasty, and in the dream I know they're what I'm supposed to eat, and I'm happy. But I've never seen blue flowers in real life. I've only seen white flowers growing in the grass down there. Are there such things as blue flowers?"

"There's all kinds of flowers!" Tomas laughed. "Blue ones, yellow ones, red and pink and green ones — hundreds of flowers! When you're free, you can eat them all!"

"No," said the llama, "I only want the blue ones. Something tells me they're the most delicious. I don't know how I know it, but I do. And I don't care if no one believes me."

Andrej turned to the wolf. "We need the keys to the cages. Is there somewhere special the zoo's owner used to keep them?"

"There is," said the wolf.

"Where? They must be close — hidden under a brick maybe, or buried in a vat of grain —"

The wolf said, "The special place where the owner kept the keys was in his coat pocket."

It took a moment for the meaning of this to sink through Andrej's mind. Then he said, "Was he wearing the coat when he went away with the lions?"

"He wore the coat everywhere he went."

Andrej nodded. He shifted his grip on the bars. "Are there spare keys? There must be."

"Of course there are," the wolf replied. "It would be unwise to have only one set of keys."

"Well then? Do you know where they are? Wolf?"

The wolf gazed at him without blinking. Andrej felt it would turn away, but it didn't. It said, "I only heard of spare keys mentioned once, by Alice to her friends. It was the night before they blew up the train, and they were excited. They'd been using the spare keys to get into the zoo for their secret meetings. That night, Alice said she mustn't forget to return the keys to the hook in the hallway of her house, where they belonged."

In his mind Andrej saw the annihilated village that lay beyond the zoo's wrought-iron fence, the houses that were no longer homes but ranges of rubble, the streets that weren't streets but repugnant obstacle courses made from the remains of lives. He laid his forehead against the bars and closed his eyes. Tomas asked, "What's happening? Andrej?"

Andrej opened his eyes. "I'm sorry," he told the wolf.

"What's going on?" asked the chamois, craning to peer past the bars.

"There are no keys," the wolf announced into the dawn.

"No keys?" The llama snorted. "Now you're being silly. No keys! There are locks, and locks have keys, so there *must* be keys. . . ."

The monkey had gone very still, its gemlike eyes darting. It looked at Andrej, at Tomas, at Wilma, and its pink lip lifted to show its white, flintlike fangs.

Then it erupted, throwing itself screaming from rope to rope, sprinting howling across the bars. It dashed to the floor and began to bang its food bowl on the stone so the metal rang earsplittingly. The kangaroo, terrified, careered into a corner and fell kicking; the llama brayed and skittered and went down on the slippery stone. The lioness rushed to the bars that separated her from the monkey and tried to force a paw through, twisting and snarling. The bear rose titanically to its full height, loosed a furious roar. Tomas pushed past Andrej and threw himself at the wolf's cage, pounding his fists on the iron. The fragile air rang with the catastrophic clangor of misery and rage and betrayal. Andrej caught at his brother's collar, yanked him off his feet. "Stop!" he shouted. "Don't do that!"

"It's not fair!" Tomas writhed. "It's not fair, it's not—"

Andrej shook him. "Stop it, I told you! The soldiers will hear!"

The monkey slammed the bowl one last time before hurling it into a corner and turning its back on the children. The kangaroo lay panting, eyes rolling to the sky; a twinge went through the coat of the collapsed llama. The bear went down on its four paws, then slumped onto the stone. Tomas's eyes were brimming with tears; when Andrej let him go he lurched about blindly, unhappy everywhere. "Andrej!" he gasped. "It's not fair! What can we do?"

"Get the baby," his brother said shortly. "You've woken her up."

Tomas mopped his face with one arm while he fished Wilma from the pack with the other, watching with tragic eyes as Andrej dug through the contents of his own pack until he found what he wanted. For the second time that night he held up to the light the corkscrew he'd discovered on the village street. "Yes!" Tomas nodded vigorously. "That's clever, Andrej!"

Bouncing the baby, he watched in complete and silent faith as Andrej slipped the corkscrew into the lock of the wolf's pen and rotated the implement artfully. The wolf edged to the center of its

cage, ears flicking to the grate of metal on metal.
When the bolt ignored the first delicate touch,
Andrej became more persuasive, jabbing and wriggling the corkscrew, pushing and shaking the gate:
yet the knuckle of iron remained unmoved, slotted
dutifully through the locking plate. Andrej swore
and stepped back, swiping the hair from his eyes.
Tomas and the animals watched as he crossed to
the seal's cage and tried again, stabbing and goug-
ing the corkscrew into the lock's innards. The
bolt remained steadfast, and something ominous
happened: the corkscrew bent like a bow. Tense
in every muscle, Andrej tried one last time, digging the sway-backed corkscrew into the lock of
the lioness's cage. The feline watched him leerily,
ears flattened to her head. Tomas couldn't bear to
see his brother doing his best, and failing: when
Andrej's shoulders dropped he hurried to say, "It
doesn't matter Andrej, it isn't your fault! We'll think
of another way . . ."

Ferocious with failure, Andrej kicked the earth,
flinging the corkscrew into the grass. The stupid

war, the stupid soldiers, the stupid corkscrew, the stupid keys: everything conspired against him, everything worked to defeat him. He pressed his body against the bars, feeling tired to the core of his bones. Tired of dodging and hiding, tired of being blown about by chance. Tired of worrying, of making decisions, of being responsible, of being forced to endure. Tired of having things taken from him. Tired by the heaviness of his heart.

The iron was so cold that it seared his skin. His boots were damp, his stomach empty, his hair tangled and his head sore. When he closed his eyes he saw not the blackness of night but the milky light of yet another day, unfeeling as a mountain, remorseless as a whipping. *Help me*, he prayed. *That's my wish.*

He listened and heard nothing, no breathing or voice or footfall, not even the whisper of leaves. It was unexpectedly lovely and restful, that moment of nothing but quiet. Opening his eyes, Andrej met the eyes of the lioness. For an instant she seemed someone else. Turning from her, he announced, "We'll stay too. If none of you can leave, we won't either."

Tomas caught a shocked breath. The animals simply gazed. "Andrej," said the lioness, "your mother told you to run."

Andrej spun to her. "I know. But she must have meant for us to run *somewhere*. When we were on the road, I didn't know where we were going. I thought we were walking where the road took us, and letting whatever happened happen. I thought we were walking nowhere. But maybe I was wrong. Maybe we were walking *here*. Maybe Mama meant for us to *run here*. Maybe *this* is the space Tomas and I are meant to fill."

"It's true," Tomas piped up. "If Mama is searching for us, this is where she'll come."

The lioness gave the children a long look, her serpentine tail flipping. Andrej stood defiant under her stare. *Every war is everyone's war, lioness*, he wanted to say. *Every life is everyone's battle*. What he said was, "We'll stay here, and we'll look after you. We'll find somewhere to hide if the soldiers come. We'll find food and water and straw for you, and things for you to play with. We'll bring sand-bags to protect you from bombs, and put roofs on your cages so the weather doesn't get in. We'll use timber to build walls for you, so you can have pri-vacy. But mostly what we'll do is *search*. We'll search for hacksaws to cut through the bars, or crowbars to pull them apart. And we'll search for the spare keys. They must be somewhere. We'll search every street until we find the owner's house, and then we'll search the house even if it's just a pile of stones: the keys will be there. I don't know how long it will take—maybe a day or a month, maybe a whole year—but we can do it, lioness. I *want* to do it."

Tomas declared, "I would *rather* do that, than do anything else."

"How nice for you!" bleated the chamois bale-fully. "To while away your life doing exactly what you want! Pity about those of us who can't! The boar is right: people are all the same. First we were prisoners of the zoo's owner, and now we're prisoners of two boys. The owner said he'd come back, but he didn't. You say you'll find the keys, but you won't. You'll search a little, but then you'll get bored, and then you'll disappear like everyone else."

The handsome goatlike beast stood glowering, its horns glinting ebony in the light. The other animals looked from it to Andrej, who eyed his challenger with dignity and said, "That's not true, chamois. Maybe I haven't got the keys in my hand, but I *do* already have them. All I need to do is find them—and I will. Finding them will be the easy part. You wait and see."

"Pshaw! Pretty talk!"

"*I* believe you," said the kangaroo. "I think you'll find the keys."

"So do I," said the bear. "I believe you."

"What will happen then?" asked the llama.

Andrej said, "I'll tell you what will happen then."

The chamois, disgusted, retreated into the shadows. Tomas shifted over to let Andrej sit on the bench, and passed Wilma to him when Andrej reached for her. Hugging the small warmth of the baby, Andrej glanced up to the sky. Three or four stars were glowing faintly there, but although the moon was gone, the sun hadn't yet arrived; and no breeze was blowing, and nothing living made a sound. For a few brief moments the land and time and life itself hung in a state of calm stasis.

Andrej shut his eyes, and thought of all the things Uncle Marin had taught him. In his memory he heard words spoken around firesides, at bedsides, along the banks of roads. In the dark, he saw the world revealed before him. In his mind, he turned the keys.

THE ESCAPE

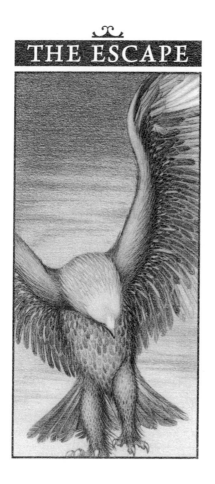

First they released the eagle. The huge bird with its pagan face watched as the gate of its cage creaked back on its hinges. It was momentarily suspicious of the big gap between the bars. But then, through the gap, it sighted a square of blue sky that was unlined by black talon marks of iron. It launched itself from its perch, and as it soared through the gate its wings spread as wide as a table. The air dislodged by the first great sweep of feathers flattened the grass of the zoo. Upward to the sun the eagle powered, spiraling on the morning air. It opened its throat and let out its cry, the sound of ice and pinnacles. Against the white sky its jet silhouette soon became no more than a speck.

They opened the other cages one by one. The bear stepped down from the stone floor, huffing as its claws met lawn. In the sunshine its auburn coat looked irresistibly warm and cuddlesome. The monkey didn't wait for its gate to open wide, but streaked chittering through the narrowest gap. Up the maple it bolted, out to the flimsiest twig. The lioness hesitated, showing her teeth to the unbarred space; she sniffed the opened doorway carefully before deciding to trust it. The seal, hearing the groan of its gate, stopped swimming and lifted its head; leaping from the water, it slid across the stone and onto the grass in one fluid and glistening movement, and propped there on its flippers. The wolf, released, leaped athletically to the grass and rolled around on its back in ecstasy. The boar poked its scruffy snout out from under the straw: sensing freedom, it emerged and shook itself spryly, trotting forward on dapper legs. The chamois butted the bars with its horns, eager to escape. It pushed through the partly open gate and ran bucking round the tree. The llama departed its cage with decorum, its soulful eyes blinking in the sun. It bent its long neck and tentatively nibbled at the grass. The kangaroo approached its open gate nervously, balancing on toes and tail. Soil under its feet made it spring joyfully, gangly limbs going everywhere.

They walked from the zoo without looking back at the cages and the mermaid and the maple and the gates that hadn't closed.

The monkey led the way for them, expertly finding a path through the wreckage of the village. They walked north, toward the mountains, passing hamlets and fording rivers, watched as they went by astonished old men and befuddled babies and invaders too flabbergasted to stop them and ask questions. Sometimes, when they rested, small children gathered round, wanting to pat the animals, believing they were pets. The lioness hunkered and snarled at them, the wolf showed its long teeth, but the llama and the monkey let themselves be caressed in return for buttered bread. They walked through villages wearied by the war, and through others that the war had ignored. They stepped past demolished houses, trod through meadows dappled by blooms. They traveled slowly, the seal and the bear setting an ambling pace, the kangaroo and monkey skipping ahead and returning to report on what lay beyond the next corner. Their mood was fine — even the wild boar's. Its exceptional nose found mushrooms and unearthed vegetables in the fields. High above, they sometimes glimpsed the eagle, its wings unfolded on a shelf of warm air.

And finally the farms and roads gave way to the stones and precipices of the mountain range.

Inside this coarse earth were buried gold, mercury and coal. Across the serrated ranges grew pristine forests of oak and fir. The wind blew cold over this taciturn country, and every slight noise — a sliding pebble, a snapping branch — rang out brittle and loud. The strange party of children and animals climbed until they reached a place from where they could see nothing but peaks and forest in every direction. Here the eagle finally disappeared into the clouds.

The lonesome mountains were home to the wolf, the boar, the chamois and the bear. Their homeland reached up through their feet and whispered in their ears, making them suddenly lawless: they did not linger to say farewell, but loped away into the undergrowth with a scatter of stone and swish of tail. If they ever saw each other again, it would be as rivals and enemies, as bears and wolves and boars and chamois have been since time immemorial. Their life together in the zoo would be a life forgotten.

The travelers, having watched them run, rested

awhile before resuming their journey, living for a time off the forest's food. Refreshed and fortified, traveling once more, they skirted small towns and great cities where the war crashed and fumed before finally and gladly reaching the tossing sea. A lengthy voyage awaited them, so they packed a raft with food. As soon as the water was deep and green and unbearably chill, the seal slipped without fanfare overboard. It disappeared into the depths, swimming fast, spinning loops, then raced back to break the surface with a spectacular leap. A white cloud reflected in its burnished eyes before it turned and vanished forever with an easy whisk of its flippers.

Their company was diminishing rapidly, but on the raft there was neither sentiment nor patience. The lioness watched as the sail was adjusted and the raft swung south, her asp of tail switching restively. The journey south was arduous, and the lioness had a cattish dislike of water; her jitteriness was compounded by the monkey's mischievous fiddling with the tiller and sail. By the time they reached the scorched sandy coast she could no longer contain herself: she pounced from the raft in horror, and charged away as fast as she could. Only when she felt the sand become dirt beneath her paws, and saw the flat green savannah stretching before her, and heard the thunder of lions calling in the distance, did she run because she was free.

Having lost sight of the lioness they turned the raft west to traverse the mighty ocean, using as their guide the invisible line of the equator. The waves here were huge, and the ceaseless plunge and swoop made the raft and its occupants groan. The voyage lasted weeks, and they told each other the same stories over and over, and played "I Spy" although there was nothing to spy until the day that land hove unannounced into view. The monkey, in a lather of excitement, behaved appallingly as the companions hiked into the jungle. It ran ahead and disappeared, it returned in time to harass the kangaroo, it plucked up spiders the size of sparrows and brandished them at the llama. Eventually it discovered a troupe of brown bald-faced monkeys exactly like itself squatting amid the branches of a tall tree. The troupe set up a clamor at the sight of the strangers; the monkey swung speedily into the tree, took a place in the branches alongside its kin, and smugly joined in the unfriendly shrieking.

Hurrying away, the depleted company crossed the continent to the open hillock country that was the llama's home. The clouds drifted low here, speckling rain; the air felt thin and oddly unsatisfying to breathe. The stony earth sprouted swards of silver spearlike grass. In the distance they sighted a herd of wild llamas with their heads raised high, gazing ruminatively at them. The llama gave a snicker of recognition, and cantered away to join them. It stood among the herd and stared back at its old comrades, and it was impossible to tell, after a minute, which of the staring llamas had been theirs.

This left only the three children and the kangaroo. Tomas crouched before its cage and asked the little creature, "Where do you live?"

"I don't know," said the kangaroo. It was lost.

Tomas looked across the lawn to his brother. "Can we keep it?"

"No," said Andrej. "Let me think." He chewed a thumbnail, trying to remember what Uncle Marin had said. *The truth of an animal is in its shape. Its body tells its truths.* "The kangaroo has a short coat, so it must come from a place where the sun shines. It has long legs for traveling, so it must be a big land. It's the color of dust, so there must be rocks and bare ground. Does that remind you of anything, kangaroo?"

The marsupial's ears swiveled, as if to the cackle of strange birds. "I think it's far. Across the sea."

"That's all right, we have the raft, we can sail anywhere."

So they steered the raft across vast worlds of water until they reached a sprawling land where the sun burned brilliantly and the kangaroo lived, and it bounded away into the haze of haggard scrub and fragrant trees, covering the ground as swiftly as a swallow cuts through the sky. "Good-bye!" Tomas called after it. "I'll miss you! Don't come back."

The haze that hung about them was not the searing sunshine of a faraway land, but the damp of coming dawn; the stone under their feet was the polished floor of cages, not a mountain's rugged side. Nevertheless the animals lay dreaming of leaves which crumpled beneath their paws, of gales that flattened their ears to their skulls, of pungent tracks and scratch marks left by others of their kind. Tomas sighed contentedly, slouching hands on hips. "Now there's just you and me and baby," he said. "What will *we* do?"

"We'll become pirates," said Andrej, putting a patch of palm over an eye. "We can sail round and round the world burying treasure and having sword fights. We'll find Uncle Marin and he can be the captain. When Wilma grows up she will be the meanest pirate of all."

"She will be!" Tomas laughed, delighted by this future. "Let's do that, Andrej. Let's be pirates."

They would not find the keys: the children and the animals knew it. But they also knew that they had no need to. They had journeyed to the final edge of life, beyond which there were no walls. The iron bars of the zoo fell away, and in their place forests sighed and sand dunes shifted, rivers flooded and mighty herds ran. Infants were born blinking and bloody, life-or-death duels were fought to the end. The sun rose and set, limbs grew stiff and tired, safe shelters were found under shadows, and eyes that had seen much but never enough fluttered and closed forever, and opened brightly again.

There was a lady standing where the pebbly path met the lawn. By the time Andrej and Tomas noticed her, the animals were already on their feet and watching her fixedly, having sensed her coming. The wolf was poking its nose between the bars. The monkey was biting its lip. The llama lifted first one foot, then another. The seal had stopped swimming.

The lady stood very still, her hands resting by her sides, a dark woolen cloak draping from her shoulders to the ground. Her face was shaded by the grayness of dawn and by the ash that the bombs had disturbed. She did not speak and they could not see her face, but Tomas knew immediately who she was: "Mama!" he cried, so surprised and pleased that he stayed where he was, fingers twined tightly together, like a good boy who knew how to behave. His mother understood about food and babies and traveling—there was nothing Mama didn't know. Certainly she would know about cages, and how to open them. His mother would care for Andrej and Wilma and himself, and everything would again be as it had always been, a life made of sunshine and roving. This battle was over, and Tomas felt joy.

It wasn't his mother, however, whom Andrej saw standing on the path. Gazing at the lady, he felt such peace overcome him that she could only be the saint, Black Sarah. From high up in the sky she must have heard his plea, must have seen that he and his siblings and the animals were in need of more than a boy—even a brave boy—could provide. With the saint at their side, no soldiers could harm them, no lightless night would confuse them, no journey would be endless or impossible. No iron bars would have the strength to resist

her will: already Andrej could hear the bolts sliding back like hands exhausted from holding on
too long. Already his own hands were opening,
reaching to take hers.

To the animals, though, the beautiful cloaked
woman who stood before them was neither mother
nor saint: she was Alice, the daughter of the zoo.
They smelled on her the caves where she'd been
hiding, the plans that she had made, the many tra-
vails she'd had to endure, the thrilling triumphs
she'd known. They smelled the reason why she
had finally come back to them, the wound that
turned her heart into a brilliant sun, a rose. *Alice*,
who didn't need a key because she bore this wound
which made of her heart an unfastened lock.

She smiled gracefully at the children, and held
out her hands to them, and in its cage the eagle
shook its wings, and readied itself to fly.